OTHER NOVELS BY THE SAME AUTHOR

Pompeii: Death Comes Calling
Whispers from Pompeii
Daughter of Pompeii

Medici: The Queen's Perfume
Cleopatra: Whispers from the Nile
Rome: The Titus Conspiracy
Arsinoe of Ephesus (Novelette)

HERCULANEUM:
Paradise Lost

Lorraine Blundell

authorHOUSE

AuthorHouse™ UK
1663 Liberty Drive
Bloomington, IN 47403 USA
www.authorhouse.co.uk
Phone: 0800 047 8203 (Domestic TFN)
+44 1908 723714 (International)

© 2020 Lorraine Blundell. All rights reserved.

No part of this book may be reproduced, stored in a retrieval system, or transmitted by any means without the written permission of the author.

Published by AuthorHouse 01/30/2020

ISBN: 978-1-7283-9818-1 (sc)
ISBN: 978-1-7283-9817-4 (e)

Print information available on the last page.

Any people depicted in stock imagery provided by Getty Images are models, and such images are being used for illustrative purposes only.
Certain stock imagery © Getty Images.

This book is printed on acid-free paper.

Because of the dynamic nature of the Internet, any web addresses or links contained in this book may have changed since publication and may no longer be valid. The views expressed in this work are solely those of the author and do not necessarily reflect the views of the publisher, and the publisher hereby disclaims any responsibility for them.

For Steve and Jenni

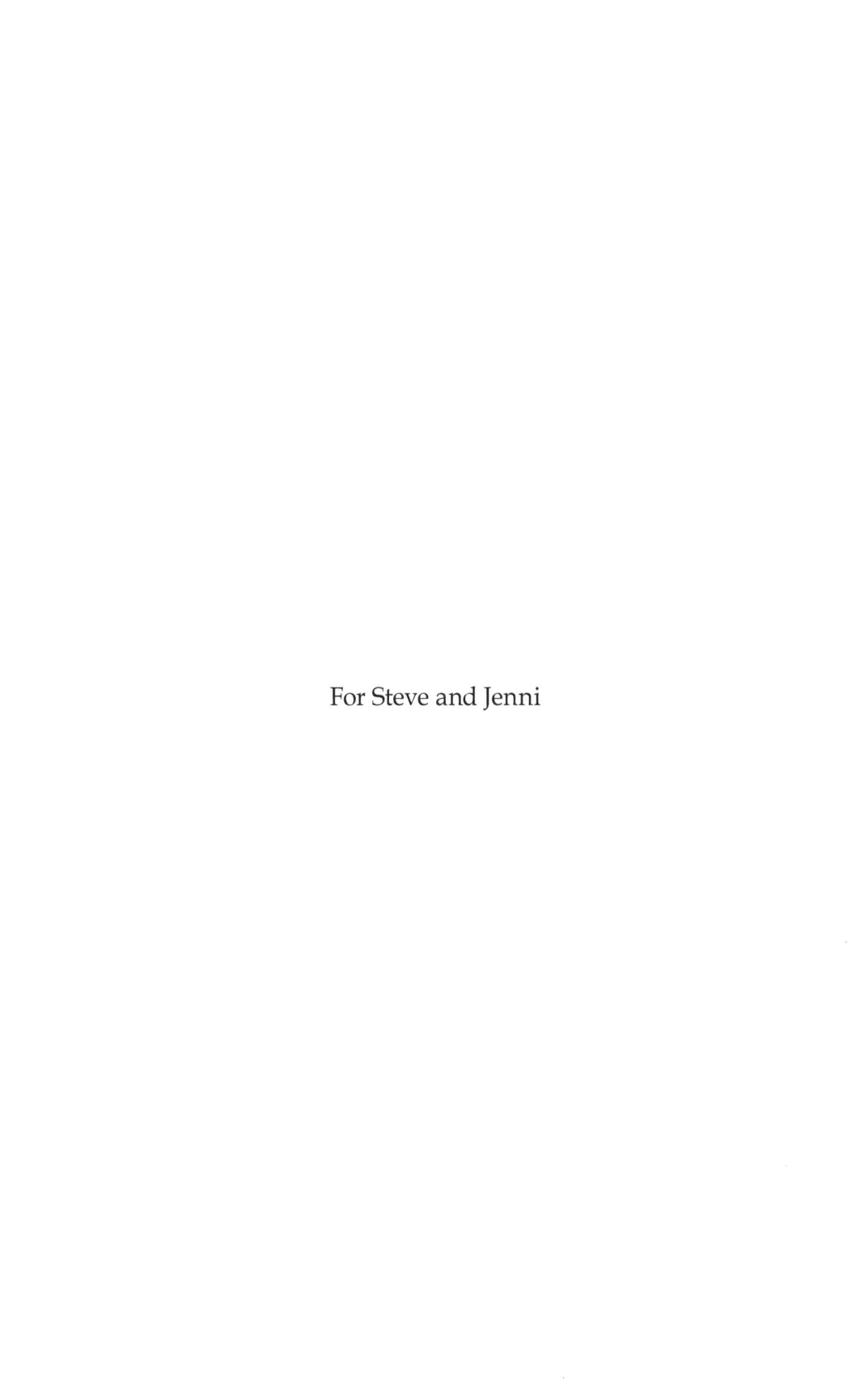

Carpe Diem...
Horace

WITH THANKS

To my daughter, Jenni, who has always been there for me with love, constant support and suggestions over the years.

Professor Miles Prince
Dr. Harold Cashmore

To Joan who brings music into my life.
To Kate who inspires me to keep writing and singing.
To Bobbie who generously gives her time to deliver books to me.

CHARACTERS

*Caesar Vespasianus Augustus   Emperor of Rome
*Titus Flavius Vespasianus   Emperor of Rome

Herculaneum

*Lucius Calpurnius Piso	Owner, Villa dei Papyri
Alexus	Greek dealer in antiques
*Prima	Elite courtesan
Aquilius Publicus	Magistrate
Sabina	His daughter
Leia	Calpurnius' slave
Frontius	Master fresco artist
Silvanus	Caretaker
Cassia	Owner of the town's hotel

*Vennidius Ennychus	Owner, the house of the Black Saloon
Livia	His wife
Florina	Her best friend & owner of the House of the Stags
Lentullus	Owner, House of the Mosaic Atrium
Spurius	Petty thief
*Julia Felix	Pompeii. Property owner

Other Minor characters

Rome

Cletus	Roman military spy
*Matidius Patrunius	Roman Senator
*Scribonius Amerinus	Roman Senator
Quintus	A criminal
Atticus	A criminal
Darius	A homeless boy

Other Minor Characters

Egypt

*Cassianus Priscus	Prefect of Egypt
Vita	His daughter
Flavius	Praetorian

* An historical character

PROLOGUE

HERCULANEUM

79 A.D.

The Necropolis
(Outside the town walls)

T he murder was easy.
It had already been carried out by the killer.
It was the disposal of the body by moonlight that proved to be much more demanding. Large and difficult to manoeuvre, the dead-weight was finally loaded into the cart. Night had fallen casting shadows over the ancient, ravaged headstones as they trundled towards the place of burial.

Nothing stirred.

Sweat ran down the faces of the two men.

'We should never have agreed to do the job,' Quintus complained.

'Bring the body here and dig the grave you mean?' Atticus queried.

'Of course, that's what I mean! What else?' Quintus snapped.

'Then why did you say we would?' Atticus frowned, his voice surly.

'Let's just get it done and then we're out of here, all right?'

They began again to dig. When an empty, gaping hole that was the grave finally stared back at them, they wheeled the cart to it and dumped the body over the edge.

Then, they bent their backs to the task of replacing the dirt they'd painstakingly taken out. They were watched over by the only witness, an ancient mulberry tree with weeping branches that hung down as if to shelter what lay beneath.

Finally, the two men departed, leaving the dead behind them. Avoiding the light cast by the full moon that silvered everything it touched, they crept back through the town walls undetected.

The sun rose the next morning with no sign of the night's gruesome activities, except for a fresh mound of dirt in the domain of the dead.

Part I

PARADISE

1

HERCULANEUM

Villa of Lucius Calpurnius Piso
(Villa of the Papyri)

78 A.D.

The pool lay below the villa, impossibly close to the sea. Its pure, turquoise water washed in the first beams of the rising sun, provided a setting that seemed as if it had been painted with liquid gold. The dawn was fine and calm bringing with it gentle waves and a fresh breeze with the tang of the ocean, promising a perfect day to come. As the sun rose further, the dewy grass of the garden with its formal box hedges and sweet oleander trees became verdant once more.

A ribbon of sandy beach ran below the front of the pool, widening further down where it reached the town, and a couple of well-maintained boathouses stood nestled in the bushes beside the pathway that led from the villa to the pristine shoreline. A graceful ship with milky white sails was presently moored in the inlet below, where it gently rose and fell on sparkling waves. In the distance, the hazy shapes of two islands could be seen.

Above them loomed the green, fertile slopes of Vesuvius. An early warning was carried on the breeze but no one was listening on that blissfully fine morning. It came as an elusive whisper so delicate that a fall of rose petals might have blown it away. In any event, it was the last thing on the minds of the two men who met in secret in the villa on the clifftop. It was known to those who were residents of Herculaneum as the *Moonlight Villa*.

The men surveyed the scene with appreciation, their fingers resting lightly on top of the stone balcony. One was the villa's owner, Calpurnius, a man of the same name as those of his male ancestors who had preceded him. The other was an Eastern trader, Alexus. He had a typically swarthy skin, a full beard and dark eyes bright with intelligence.

'Our venture has brought us much wealth,' he smiled. 'Hopefully, we can keep it that way. You were wise to suggest basing our activities here rather than in Rome.'

'Indeed,' Calpurnius nodded in agreement. 'Fortunately, there has been no one showing any curiosity at all yet, as far as I can tell.'

'Our plan is not for the eyes of others,' his companion agreed. This is by far the safest and most secure way of conducting our business. I have a gift for you today for your library.' Alexus reached into his outer garments and drew out a scroll which he handed to his friend.

Intrigued, Calpurnius opened it. It was a rare work written by an ancient poet, and very precious. 'My thanks, Alexus, you are indeed generous.'

Calpurnius was by far the younger of the two men and

undeniably handsome. His smiling blue eyes and fair hair were characteristic of family members who'd come before him, while he owed his physique and erect bearing to his past military service under Nero. He was young to have resigned his commission in the army.

They walked slowly across the intricate mosaic floor of the atrium towards the villa's main reception room, Calpurnius slowing his steps to allow Alexus to limp along beside him. The Greek no longer noticed his restricted movement resulting from an altercation long ago in a narrow alleyway in Athens. Seating himself comfortably Alexus studied the rich red floor rug, exquisite frescoes and coloured inlaid marble that adorned the room, resulting in a beauty that spoke of great wealth.

'Yes, we will both do rather well from our endeavours,' Alexus said softly, gesturing expansively at the room around him as he fingered his beard while mentally calculating the worth of each item.

'I asked you here today to discuss the future,' Calpurnius explained. 'We need to have more stock. We must continuously have something new to show our clients in Baiae or they will look elsewhere to buy.'

Alexus' glance fell upon a large fresco covering the whole wall in front of him. He was silent momentarily before remarking. 'This wasn't here last time I came, Calpurnius, if my memory is accurate?'

'Stunning, isn't it!'

'Yes. It occurs to me that your beautiful model is worthy of more than just this fresco. I've rarely seen a more captivating young woman. And we need to produce some new statues to entice customers to part with their money, don't you think?'

Alexus raised a questioning eyebrow.

'She would make a seductive Venus, I agree.'

'We could attribute it as being a previously unknown Praxiteles,' Alexus suggested, rubbing his hands together. 'If we add a few new busts and other statues as well that should be enough, at least for the near future.'

'I believe so,' Calpurnius replied. 'I'll find out the model's name,' he added, 'and she can pose for my best sculptor. We should be able to come up with statues that rich Roman senators and wealthy matrons can't wait to show off in their gardens.'

The two men laughed as they relaxed with cups of wine, well pleased with their decision. The fragrance of jasmine suffused the air.

'Are you not lonely here, alone?' The old Greek glanced at his friend. His expression as he did so was both curious and a little sad. 'I have the company of my wife and children and many would be surprised to learn of a pretty young woman whose company I seek from time to time. My life is full and pleasurable.'

He paused, waiting for Calpurnius to speak.

'My life has been one of duty until now,' he explained. 'In many ways it still is,' he continued but did not elaborate. 'It isn't easy in Rome's army to reach the rank of tribune. I own a beautiful slave whose company I find fulfilling and I also have this wonderful estate.

Most of all, I enjoy possessing rare and beautiful creations of literature and art. I must admit to you though,' Calpurnius' voice was thoughtful, 'I worry that I don't have an heir to follow me. He must be my legitimate or adopted son, of course. There can be no question about his birth. The problem is that I don't have any desire to marry right now.'

'Then, most certainly, my friend, you should not do so. You will undoubtedly know when you're ready,' Alexus counselled him.

They talked on together, two old friends enjoying each other's company, until the day was nearly spent. Each looked forward to what the future might offer.

Alexus boarded his ship as the sun set and the waters below the villa lay unoccupied once more. Calpurnius watched his friend leave until the ship was barely a white dot on the horizon. Later, as evening fell, he smiled to himself as he strolled through the colonnade of the villa's inner peristyle, passing into the garden beyond with its long pool and precious, original sculptures of water carriers. This villa and its contents were worth a fortune. Only master craftsmen had worked on its luxurious mosaic floors and furnishings. Walls of rich crimson met the eye of the beholder. It was a place of great beauty and comfort.

Calpurnius settled himself on one of the benches to relax. The young woman in the large fresco was indeed stunningly beautiful. The painting had been completed during his recent, short absence in Rome. That had confirmed the wisdom of his choice to resign from the army, as he studied the chaos that was left after Nero's suicide and the year that had followed, leaving Vespasian to bring Rome and the Empire back to normality.

The more he thought about the model the more Lucius determined that he would certainly use her again. Alexus was clearly an admirer, and Calpurnius had found in the past that he was clever when it came to business. Also, the old fresco painter, Frontius, had praised her as the only woman worthy of being portrayed as a goddess and his instincts were usually sound.

In his imagination Calpurnius could hear the clink of gleaming gold coins running through his fingers from the pouches of the eager, gullible purchasers of copies of the new statue. It wasn't that he was avaricious, but there were secrets and promises he had to keep that required wealth for reasons that must remain hidden. For the moment he needed it to stay that way.

He called the young slave Leia to him.

'Yes, Dominus?' she whispered as she knelt before him her head bowed.

Calpurnius stroked her long, raven-coloured hair. 'I missed you when I was in Rome,' he told her. 'It's been a busy day, bring me another cup of wine. Later, you can go to my room and wait for me.'

Leia looked up admiringly at Calpurnius then quietly left him. She'd long ago fallen in love with her master despite being only too aware of the hopelessness of her situation. He was gentle and generous with her and she knew she was indeed fortunate to belong to him.

Later, at dinner, Calpurnius dined alone, fully satisfied after a fulfilling interlude with Leia and excellent food from the villa's kitchen. His thoughts went back over the years. Much had happened in that time. Then, he dozed in his chair.

Night fell, obliterating all outside sight of the great villa that ran along the clifftop perched high above the sea on the fringe of Herculaneum. Inside, the discrete glow of oil lamps cast pools of welcome light, but in the shadows the villa clung to its secrets hidden behind a veil of deception.

The next morning at dawn Calpurnius strolled alone on the beach in front of the villa. Nothing moved except for a cooling breeze that tousled his hair. He walked barefoot, his feet scrunching into the gritty sand. Sitting down on the grassy bank, he leaned back against an old, broken tree trunk behind him and gazed with pleasure at the paradise that surrounded him.

And it was all his!

Life as a tribune in Rome's army had been both stimulating and challenging, providing him with camaraderie and a level of respect to which he'd grown accustomed. The timing to leave, however, had been right when he'd received news that he'd been gifted this estate in the will of a deceased ancestor. His was an illustrious family with a proud heritage.

Calpurnius had just about everything any man could want, but an insatiable drive to use his position for the good of

Rome's people drove him on. For now, he planned to increase his wealth and power not only for the comforts of life that it provided for him, but also until he needed to call upon it for Rome.

2

ASIA MINOR

78 A.D.

Sardis
(Turkey)

After leaving Calpurnius' villa, Alexus sailed on calm seas straight to the safe anchorage of the large and impressive city of Ephesus which was under Roman rule. He liked this city, so well-known to Antony and Cleopatra as well as her unfortunate half-sister, Arsinoe. This was the second largest and most prosperous city in the Roman Empire, but it had an individual character all its own.

He paused for a few moments of contemplation upon reaching the marble mausoleum of Arsinoe, on the hill at the top of Arcadian Street. She'd been murdered by Antony at Cleopatra's insistence.

Alexis enjoyed sea travel but he was well aware that in this, he was somewhat unusual. His actual destination was not far away from Ephesus. It was the well-known trading centre of Sardis.

The day was hot and dusty when he finally arrived.

The popular town market on the main road buzzed with activity. It was a road in use even from far more ancient times. Many visitors made their way to the adjacent temple of Artemis to pray to the goddess. Fervently, they bowed their heads oblivious to the ruckus around them.

Alexus heard a number of different languages spoken, and various street food kiosks supplied a variety of different cultural food offerings as well as flowers and fruit.

He passed one old woman intently studying the vibrant, red pomegranates offered to her for inspection at a stall. Her face was lined from years of living. In her basket already lay the figs she'd purchased. She glanced up at him with an expression of curiosity then shuffled away.

Fragrances from incense, blossoms and spices wafted from the temple as they floated across the crowds, and the babble of speech presented an alluring picture of a large, vibrant marketplace. Here, valuable trading pieces from Persia, Greece, Rome and occasionally, Egypt, collided. There were plenty of treasures to be had if one had the money.

And Alexus did.

He entered the various tents that clustered together, their owners calling to travellers to inspect their stock. He stared intently at the marble statues, busts, aromatic cedarwood tables and other classical pieces around him, assessing their quality and worth, as he moved from tent to tent. He was acutely aware that the business he shared with Calpurnius was growing larger very quickly. It was time, once more, to provide him with something really special - something that was as unique as Alexus could find.

If Calpurnius liked what Alexus gave him enough, then he would give it to his friend as a gift rather than a business purchase. The two men had formed a lasting friendship over the years. Their liking for each other was genuine.

'A refreshing drink for you?' the owner of the present tent and its offerings asked with a bow.

'Yes, if you please.'

Alexus could see from his clothing and hear from his accented Greek, that the owner was an Arab who on meeting him, had correctly deduced that Alexus was Greek and switched immediately to speaking his language instead.

The Arabs in Sardis had a reputation for reasonable and fair dealing, especially if they respected the customer. They were clever and had creative ways of finding goods of real quality. The tent was large with a considerable amount of stock.

'Please, take as much time as you require,' the owner offered pleasantly as he retreated to give Alexis privacy.

He began to wander through the items on offer. It was possible that he could buy something in nearby Ephesus, but the really good trading was to be done here, he knew, where it was a major speciality of the town rather than that of a religious centre.

Carefully, he studied each piece and was about to leave without buying, when he noticed in a corner a headless female statue with wings. He was drawn to it like a magnet. It was unique. This one was not a statue of the usual kind of goddess that he supplied to Calpurnius, but, rather, one the like of which as far as he was aware had never been seen before.

'Where did this come from?' he enquired curiously of the owner as he ran his fingers over the graceful, fluid folds of the wings.

'I'm told it was pulled from the sands of a Greek island

called Samothrace,' he replied. 'Here, I'll bring the statue forward so you can study it more closely, it's very old.'

The originality, feeling of fluidity of movement and grace fascinated Alexus. He knew that he'd found the gift he was looking for. He turned to the trader. 'I'll buy it. My men will come for it this afternoon. Great care must be taken to protect this statue.'

Having paid the price after a little haggling, Alexus left with a spring in his step. Would Calpurnius ever be able to bring himself to actually sell this original? He thought not, although he could, or course, have it copied. Then again, where would a sculptor be found who could do this statue justice?

On returning to Ephesus, Alexus visited the bathhouse where he also enjoyed a massage. The wealth of the city was evident in the marble buildings and size of the establishments. For a while Alexus soaked in the warmth of the water, pleased with himself because of the purchase he'd just made. The bottom of the pool was as blue as the sea, highlighted by the artistic, mosaic floor of the same colour which was decorated with playful dolphins.

Slaves attended expertly to his every need.

'You should be less firm,' Alexus ordered the huge man who was pounding him as he lay on the massage table.

'As you wish, Dominus.'

On leaving, Alexus walked the short distance into the most well-known brothel in the centre of the city. It stood of the corner of Marble Street. The girls from whom he made his choice came from many different places. After careful consideration, Alexus chose a young, slim woman of oriental appearance with shiny, dark hair that hung down her back. He liked her shy smile.

Her name was Amina. She was gentle and eager to please.

Afterwards, he walked down Marble Street fully relaxed

and satisfied. His tiredness had gone, to be replaced by contentment.

The shouts of excitement coming from that afternoon's gladiator games nearby in the huge theatre, rose to fever pitch around him. He considered going in to watch for a while, but then decided to continue on his way instead. He'd be sure to go to Rome, the centre of gladiator games, next time he travelled. With any luck he'd be able to enjoy the spectacle of the Games in Vespasian's new amphitheatre. But, to build it would take time.

Alexis felt he'd had enough of journeying from place to place for the moment. He walked at a leisurely pace down to the harbour to where his ship lay at anchor, then he sat relaxing while he drank one of the finest wines he'd ever tasted.

The next day, after the statue had been delivered to him and checked for damage, he ordered his crew to sail back to Athens. His home there was palatial and contained many exotic pieces from his travels. In this, it was similar to Calpurnius' villa.

When he arrived, the house in the sunlight was brilliantly white under a cloudless and flawless blue sky but it was shaded and restful, due to numerous cypress trees and fountains gurgling water. Pathways were still and quiet places of peace and the air was full of the fresh scent of pine. The servants were reserved and experienced, their virtually silent footfalls almost soundless. Alexus had always felt that the house and gardens held the smell of summer in them and it relaxed him.

'We're all so happy to have you back!' his senior servant bowed before him, offering cheese and olives.

'It's good to *be* back,' Alexus smiled. 'I've missed being home lately.'

Alexis had been born into a comfortable although not rich family in Athens. His younger sister was fortunate to be very attractive as well as sweet-tempered and she'd married into one of the richest families in the city.

He was a wealthy man in his own right, after a lifetime of

pursuing antiques of great beauty. He was steeped in culture and learning so he loved to travel, but he was tired and realised that he was feeling his age. Alexus made the decision to remain at home resting and visiting his family for a considerable period of time. Later, he'd venture away again. Then, he'd take the statue he'd bought to Calpurnius in Herculaneum.

3

HERCULANEUM

In the inky depths of a still night a roman boat approached the inlet beneath the Piso villa in Herculaneum. A solitary man holding a flare stood on the narrow strip of beach, aiding its approach with his guiding light. A gentle swish of waves on the calm sea proved ideal for an effortless and virtually silent arrival, as the boat dipped into and out of the shadows.

Calpurnius stood back closer to the villa until the centurion approached him. Briskly, they strode towards each other.

'Good evening, Marcus.'

'It's good to see you again, Calpurnius. Vespasian sends you greetings and his thanks,' the centurion responded.

Behind them, legionaries carried heavy chests the last few steps from the water and onto the beach. The soldiers, hand-picked for the assignment and sworn to secrecy, struggled under the weight.

'How many chests do we have?' Calpurnius asked.

'There are five tonight. They're loaded right to the top,' Marcus explained in a low voice as he gestured towards his men to pick up the chests again and follow him.

Not for the first time, Lucius was grateful for the door that led into the villa's lower basement area. It was the size of a small room with no entry from the rest of the villa, except through a locked door on the back wall. The room's exterior, covered with ivy and bushes was well concealed.

The legionaries entered and stacked the chests on top of those already there. By the light of the flare, Calpurnius, having carefully counted the total number of chests inside the room, locked the door behind them after they'd finished, then signed the document that Marcus held out to him.

'Let me know next time you're visiting Rome and we can have dinner together,' Marcus invited as the two men clasped hands and he retreated back towards the water.

'Farewell, my friend, may the gods go with you,' Calpurnius replied, his smile lost in the darkness.

He stood on the beach watching until he was once again alone except for the caretaker who held the flair.

Silvanus had been with Calpurnius ever since he'd become owner of the villa, having resigned at the same time from the army. They'd seen tough fighting action together which had resulted in Silvanus permanently carrying an injury which left him with one of his arms weaker than the other. His loyalty to Calpurnius was absolute. He acted as caretaker for the estate.

'Sir,' he began, 'I've locked the front gate and checked on the security of the villa, is there anything else you'd like me to do?'

'No thanks, Silvanus, I told Leia to retire and I believe it's time at this hour of the night, that both of us did the same. Goodnight.'

'Goodnight, sir.'

Silvanus made his way to the small cottage that he lived in not far from the main gate. He was close enough to it to hear anyone attempting to enter. Although the cottage was tiny, it included a bedroom, a small kitchen and wash area, and a place to sit near the window. It was comfortable. He took his meals provided for him with Leia and the gardener in the kitchen at the villa.

The cook was a middle-aged woman from the town who came to the villa daily to prepare meals and ensure that the kitchen was efficiently run. She'd been a cook in one of the wealthy villas in Rome several years ago, so she was much more skilful than merely competent. It was not unusual to find dishes such as stuffed nightingales' tongues or other delicacies on the table.

Silvanus was grateful for the quality of life he had, now that he was no longer fit for active army duty. He'd wondered what was to become of him until he'd been offered the caretaker's position. It was not really friendship that he felt for Calpurnius, they were, at least in his eyes, too far removed in importance for that, but rather, respect, loyalty and gratitude.

Silvanus needed no reminding from Calpurnius, that what he'd seen tonight and other nights, as well as matters of a personal nature concerning the master of the villa, were private. In fact, as far as he was concerned, they had never happened.

Up in the villa Leia vaguely heard the arrival of the boat on the beach, then turned over and went back to sleep. Later, Calpurnius tiredly pulled the bed covers over himself and settled into the comfort of the expensive bed that echoed the quality of the furniture and fittings in his bedroom. He lay thinking about the latest delivery of gold that sat in his cellar. Not even Leia knew about it. There was no reason to believe that there would ever be any risk of discovery.

He considered the agreement he'd made secretly with the Emperor, Vespasian. He'd been taken on a tour of the start of construction of the huge new amphitheatre that was being built in Rome. Vespasian was struggling for funds to build it, even allowing for the large amount of gold being transported to Rome from the victory in Judea.

A construction of this huge size required gold without measure. But the Emperor considered that it was worth it!

The Roman people were discontented after the chaotic reign of Nero and the year that had followed his suicide. Calpurnius was of the opinion, that it was sheer genius by Vespasian to provide them with entertainment the like of which they'd never seen. Such an enterprise, however, had also never before been attempted.

His existing activities with his friend, Alexus, based in his villa in Herculaneum, had become a cover also, for the needs of Rome's emperor, Vespasian.

Calpurnius was in the midst of massively increasing his business providing the wealthy of Rome with much admired copies of precious Greek sculptures.

He and Alexus each kept an agreed percentage of the proceeds from incoming finances. The remainder was funnelled through to Vespasian.

Alexus brought priceless marble statues and busts from Greece as his part of the bargain, or sometimes, even a particularly eye-catching rug from Persia.

A highly skilled artisan was all that was needed to sculpt one copy of each statue. They were then transported to Calpurnius' sculpture factory further along the coast in Baiae and if necessary, duplicated again there as often as required.

The gold from the undertaking, presently sitting in Calpurnius' cellar, was held for Vespasian in secret, until he needed it to complete the Flavian Amphitheatre if Rome's treasury ran low. He was as close to certain as it was possible to be, he informed Calpurnius, that his fears would not turn into reality. However, one never really knew.

The Emperor considered it unwise, to take any risk that citizens could become aware that the holdings of Rome's treasury were low due to the stadium's construction. He had no wish to have a riot on his hands.

Once they'd experienced the entertainment it offered, that would cease to matter, but considerable time would necessarily elapse before the amphitheatre could be totally finished and ready to work its magic.

Apart from his inner satisfaction at being able to contribute, Calpurnius' reward was a grateful emperor. He saw no moral dilemma in the type of business that he and Alexus ran.

He'd seen too much corruption so rampant in Rome's elite wealthy to worry about it, especially as this project was largely being undertaken for the good of the Roman people and the stability of the Empire. It did not occur to him to doubt Vespasian's decision to use the gold to build the stadium of death he'd decided on.

Calpurnius knew his place. He drifted off into a peaceful sleep content with his decision.

4

A Thermopolium

The following morning promised to be another glorious day in the small, wealthy seaside resort of Herculaneum. The sun rose with shades of gold and pink over tall palm trees swaying gently in a slight breeze. It gave light to an orderly, clean town laid out in a formal grid pattern in which it was easy to see the ancient Greek influence of its past.

Skilled artisans, fishermen and lawyers usually did well in the town, but there was little in the way of large-scale production and exporting of goods such as the famous garum sauce made from rotting fish guts, sold by Umbricius Scaurus in Pompeii.

The main attraction of Herculaneum was its seaside location with palm trees, as well as its gracious, quiet atmosphere linked with houses, temples and public buildings of artistic beauty. And then, there was the ongoing enchantment of sea and sand.

Herculaneum was much quieter than Pompeii, with more wealth and an opinion of itself as being very much more sophisticated. Many Pompeians weren't sure that they really liked the inhabitants who came from the smaller town of Herculaneum barely a short ride away.

Arrogance was the usual complaint about its residents. The dislike wasn't enough, however, to deter those from Pompeii investing to make money from property transactions in Herculaneum.

Julia Paris had successfully invested in two houses side by side in central Herculaneum. Some months later, she sold one of them to a gentleman by the name of Dama. Her profit had been considerable and she was content, even though she knew she'd never be as wealthy as Julia Felix, a well-known entrepreneur from Pompeii.

The houses along the foreshore that looked out over the sand on the shoreline were worth a great deal of money. As was usual with property, the houses in the streets behind it were less valuable and varied in price depending on their location.

On this morning, a young man by the name of Decius, sat on a familiar stool at his favourite thermopolium. He looked out across the bay as he watched fishermen with their nets full from many hours coaxing delectable seafood from the sea. They were now returning to the beach. He sniffed at the sharp, distinctive smell of the ocean in appreciation, then ordered his pastry for breakfast, as he considered the sculpting he planned to complete by the time sunset came around.

Decius had been a sculptor all his life. His father had been highly skilled and ensured that his son learned all he needed to know to excel in his trade. It certainly wasn't by accident that he was much sought after not only in his home town but also in Pompeii nearby. He believed that he could look forward to a comfortable future and unlike most of the residents of Herculaneum, who were either freedmen or slaves, he was freeborn.

'Do you have a busy day ahead?' Decius asked the shop owner, his friend, Justus. 'I imagine your days are full of plenty of customers wanting their wine and beef stew?' It was too early for other customers to arrive yet, so Justus was leaning casually over the bar counter, his arms resting comfortably on top.

'The same as always,' Justus muttered, bored. 'Things will get busy around lunch hour I expect. And what about you, Decius?' his friend asked. 'I guess you have to wait sometimes for a while before an order for a bust or garden herm comes in?'

Their conversation was cut short before he could answer as Decius looked up to see the tall figure of Calpurnius Piso walking briskly down the street towards them. He wasn't really surprised. Despite his wealth and respected reputation, Calpurnius was often to be seen in town amongst the citizens and was well liked.

Generous and pleasant but firm when necessary, he was a patron of the town's theatre, and also gave generously to purchase awards for presentations to the winners in athletic competitions such as throwing, frequently held in the Palaestra. It was a large communal area shaded with trees around its perimeter.

Easing himself off his stool with a slight nod at Justus, Decius was standing by the time Herculaneum's most wealthy and influential resident reached him.

'I thought I'd find you here. Salve, Decius.'

'Salve, sir.'

'You look well,' Calpurnius remarked. 'I'm wondering if you have time to undertake an important and rather urgent commission for me?'

Decius didn't hesitate. He had other work, but whatever it was Calpurnius wanted, he would pay far better. The other jobs could wait. Besides, he loved sculpting the high -quality statues and busts that only Calpurnius usually required.

'When would you like me to begin, sir?'

'Tomorrow morning, if you can manage it. I'm hoping that the model will also be free then. If not, I'll send a message to let you know.'

'Thank you, sir.'

Calpurnius nodded and retreated back the way he'd come. He enjoyed leisurely early morning walks beside the sea. It was so different from the army life he'd lived until recent years, and he genuinely enjoyed meeting and spending time with the town's people. They'd taken some time to accept him, as is common in any small town, but once they did, they found that they liked him.

Calpurnius was a leader of men. He was courageous in battle and intelligent. These qualities were recognised early in his army career and had led to quick promotion. He was also a man who could be trusted. His word was his bond. He'd never seen anything like the huge amphitheatre that Vespasian had begun to build.

'Well, looks like you've got some work coming your way,' Justus grinned as they watched Calpurnius retrace his steps. 'I wish I had wealthy customers, but I suppose that wouldn't help much, given that beef stew will always be just beef stew!'

'At least you'll still have me as a customer,' Decius reassured him with a smile. 'I suppose that's not much comfort, but it's the best I can do.' He left the thermopolium and made his way back to visit the first customer on his list for the day.

Calpurnius had no wish to be late for the meeting of the town council listed to be held later this morning. He quickened his steps accordingly. A handful of influential men held in their hands the power to make important decisions to maintain and improve the life of Herculaneum's citizens. They were all wealthy and respected.

The House of the Mosaic Atrium
Cardo IV

The House of the Mosaic Atrium stood next to the House of the Stags amongst the palm trees. Stunningly located, these houses had some of the best views in the town, right on the foreshore.

'Salve. Please come in,' the porter welcomed Calpurnius when he rang for entry.

He was led through the enormous atrium with its marble impluvium to the main reception room, a place with which he was familiar. Today, it was the turn of the master of the house, Lentullus, to chair the meeting. The three other councillors, Sirius, Aelius and the magistrate, Aquilius, were already sitting waiting.

'How are you, Calpurnius?' Aelius asked in greeting.

'I'm always busy. But of course, we are none of us ever content, are we?' he replied. 'Either there is too much to do or not enough!'

Aelius shrugged. 'You're right, of course.'

'I call the meeting to order! Now to the main problem we need to do something about today,' declared Lentullus. 'I've had complaints that mausoleums and graves in the main Necropolis outside the walls have been vandalised.' He waited for his words to register with the others.

'To what extent?' queried Sirius.

'Quite considerably.'

Aquilius frowned. 'Who can have had such little respect for the dead?' he paused to let his words take effect. 'And for that matter, for the law?'

'Do we have the funds in the community chest to repair them?' Aelius asked.

'I believe so. But that's not the main problem,' Lentullus continued. 'How do we stop the same thing from happening again?'

'We must catch the person responsible,' replied the

magistrate, Aquilius, curtly. 'Leave it with me. I'll report back to you at the next meeting.'

After a pleasant enough discussion of other more trivial matters, the meeting soon ended and the councillors retreated to the vast garden, colourful and fragrant, to enjoy refreshments whilst relaxing to the ever-present sound of the sea in their ears.

III

After the meeting had broken up, Aquilius walked alone at a sedate pace through the town towards the necropolis. As was his usual practice, he looked around him as he went, attentively checking for anything out of order.

He was a man of middle age with a pleasant appearance.

The town council was particularly against littering, for which a slave could expect a good flogging, while those who were free were issued with a stiff fine. So, obviously, damage such as had apparently been done to graves in the city necropolis, required immediate investigation.

Aquilius felt the sun's warmth on his face and enjoyed his walk until he reached the town Gate. His pace slowed, and his mood became more sombre as he passed through to the first of several mausoleums and came to the damage, which was obvious. He felt sure that the gods would ensure that the culprits paid for their malicious actions, however, he also wanted to catch them in this life, as soon as possible.

He stopped as each tombstone was reached, if he knew the occupant. It occurred to him that many had died more years ago than he'd realised. Some gravestones were untended and ravaged by time, the wind and rain lashing them and the green moss clinging to the stone, invading the engraved surfaces.

How quickly time passed!

Eventually, Aquilius reached the headstone of his beloved wife, noting with relief that it had not been damaged. She'd never been strong, so it was not totally unexpected when many years ago, she'd succumbed to a cough in a particularly cold winter, leaving him with a young daughter to raise alone.

He spoke softly to her now, as he always did, where she lay below the earth. He hoped that she could hear him. *Sabina is a beautiful young woman. You would have been proud of our daughter,* he told her sadly.

Then, soberly, as was his way, Aquilius went back along the path by which he'd come. There was work to do.

After the meeting, arriving back at his villa, Calpurnius saw the fresco painter, Frontius, sitting on the portico steps waiting for him. He sat, unmoving, enjoying the warmth of the sun. If Calpurnius had not returned when he did, the painter would undoubtedly have fallen asleep.

Mostly, Calpurnius found that residents of working age from the town were agreeable and worked hard. Whenever possible, he sourced the best of them to do whatever he needed.

The fresco painter was one of them.

'You're early, Frontius,' the villa's owner greeted the silver-haired painter. He started with surprise when spoken to.

'Yes, sir. I believe you wish to know who the model was for the large fresco I recently painted for you. I can tell you that the girl I used last time was Helena. She lives not far from the hotel. She'll probably be available if you'd like her to come. She's quite young and not very experienced, but really an easy model to work with. I think Decius will be happy with her.'

'Would you mind giving Helena a message on your way home?' Calpurnius asked amiably. 'Invite her to come early in the morning, Frontius. By the way, I'd also be pleased if you could begin work on another fresco, probably of a bowl of fruit on a table. It should have rich colours, I think, but it won't be needed until the statue is finished so we can discuss it further then.'

'Of course, sir. Thank you. I'll go and give Helena your message.' Frontius left.

Calpurnius turned to his caretaker. 'Silvanus, I'll be away for a while. Keep a particularly good watch on the estate while I'm gone,' Calpurnius told him as he patted him on the back. 'Word gets around quickly when there are less people here for protection. One never knows what some of the town's criminals will get up to. There aren't many but it only takes one or two to cause problems.'

'Of course, sir. But who should I contact if I think trouble is likely? You'll be too far away.'

'Get an urgent message to magistrate Aquilius Publicus. I've already alerted him that I'll be in Baiae for a while for business and a few days of rest. I don't really want to alert the town's residents in any way that I'll be absent, otherwise I'd employ another man to help you.'

'I'm sure all will be well,' Silvanus answered reassuringly. 'I suppose I'm still to admit Decius and Helena to work on the statue?'

'Yes, definitely. I want that finished urgently. I'll leave things in your capable hands. Salve.'

The next morning, Leia watched from a balcony as Calpurnius mounted his horse and soon disappeared from view. She knew he was an excellent rider, but travel could be dangerous. She worried whenever he was away.

Leia still had light duties, however, even though her master was gone. With a sigh, before beginning her tasks, she went to peep from a partially open door to watch Decius at work for a few minutes.

His model, Helena was young and inexperienced but very beautiful. She was known to be a gossip who always knew who came and went in the town, and the details of everyone's personal relationships, especially if they had something to hide.

Leia watched Decius for a while as he worked. She was fascinated by the way his deft crafting could possibly produce what it did from a hard block of marble.

She had no doubt from what she saw, that the statue would soon begin to look more like a stunning goddess than a lifeless slab of stone.

5

The House of the Black Saloon
Decumanis Maximus

'But it's *black*!' Livia shrieked as she stared in horror at the wall in front of her. She turned in a circle, and the sight of all the other walls of the large reception room and hallway the same colour, left her without further physical possibility of speech. Frontius' mouth hung open in shock. Never before had he witnessed such alarm from a customer. He came quickly to her side.

'You did ask for the latest fashion,' his reminded her, his voice faltering. 'This is the upcoming colour for houses of the wealthy,' he persisted in his defence. 'There are already two other houses in town with the same colour on at least one wall.'

'Are they on a main street like ours?'

'Well, no.'

'Are they as large and impressive as this one?'
'No, but…'
Livia interrupted him. 'My husband is not going to like this!' she declared emphatically, shaking her head. It was apparent that she'd completely disregarded the lovely artistic frieze features the painter had also placed on the wall, adding shades of gold and red that offset the stark blackness.

Vennidius Ennychus was a surly man with a reputation for being difficult to deal with and Frontius had no wish to upset him. He wondered how he was going to get out of this mess.

Suddenly, Livia ran from the room. A terrible thought had occurred to her. Frontius hurried after her in alarm.

'Thank the gods!' she exclaimed as she stared at the walls of the bedrooms which remained with a white background. 'For one dreadful moment I thought you might have painted these too.'

'You only asked for the reception room,' Frontius blurted out before he had time to consider the wisdom of his remarks, 'but if you change your mind I can always come back and paint these rooms too,' he added hopefully. 'Perhaps a totally different colour?'

Livia glared at him. 'Get out! I don't want to see you again. You'll be fortunate if you don't hear from Vennidius about this! I've got no intention of paying you for what you've left us with!'

'But you have to pay for the work I've done,' Frontius gasped. 'What about the cost of the paint and then there's my time on top of that. It's not my fault you left it to me to choose a colour and then didn't like it.'

Livia said nothing more. She flounced from the room making her way to the nearby peristyle where she sat, immobile, still fuming.

Frontius knew that there was no way she was going to change her mind, not yet, anyway, so he gathered up a couple of remaining paint containers and quickly made his way out the door. That was one customer who wouldn't be asking for his services again for some time, if ever. He sighed in frustration. He was determined, though, that the bill would be paid. He'd be raising the matter again with Livia and her husband once the situation had cooled down.

Frontius decided that he should probably go home for the remainder of the day, or perhaps more appropriately, to the nearby bar. He was certainly in no mood to do more painting. The empty paint containers clattered as he threw them hastily into the back of his handcart and left.

Lately, he'd begun to worry that he was becoming older and that the money he had to last him through old age and illness, was obviously not going to be enough. He didn't think it was fair that with all of the work he'd done he should end up in this position.

But life was rarely fair and he knew it. He returned the cart to where he lived then sat down in the bar and thought about his life before Herculaneum.

Frontius was a first-class fresco painter.

He'd been born in Rome to a couple who had enough money to survive on but were not really what could be called 'comfortable.' They arranged for him to undertake training with one of the city's best painters. Frontius learned quickly and it was recognised early that he possessed creative talent.

Then, unexpectedly, had come what would later be referred to as the golden age for artisans. It was an exciting time.

After the great fire of Rome, the Emperor, Nero, decided to build his dream, the *Golden Palace* over the ruins. It would be the most spectacular royal palace and pleasure gardens that the world had ever seen. To do the work, however, he needed not only labourers, but many talented artisans to undertake the glorification of the structure.

Frontius was in a perfect position to take advantage of the situation. He offered his services and was immediately accepted. He was well paid and proud of the frescoes he painted. It was whispered that the palace would stand forever and he was proud of his contribution.

But by the time the palace had been completed, Nero had committed suicide and the work had dried up. It was then that Frontius' wife walked out with all of their savings. She left him without even enough coins to buy a cup of wine.

Frontius didn't even try to find her. It was an impossible task and he knew it. He got work where he could, but found it difficult to meet the cost of his room in the insula where he lived.

Then the beginning of the construction of Vespasian's new amphitheatre gave him some work once again for a short time. But as Frontius began to realise how much he was struggling to survive because the work was not permanent, he knew that he'd be better off in a quiet place away from Rome.

He hadn't been working at the amphitheatre more than a few weeks before he decided that it would be best if he left. His main problem was low morale caused by recent events. He needed to leave the location which held such upsetting memories for him.

One day, he simply packed up his belongings and went.

Frontius chose to settle in Herculaneum.

The House with the Beautiful Courtyard
Cardo IV

Frontius rented a top floor apartment in Herculaneum which perfectly suited his needs. The house had a beautiful courtyard which had steps leading upwards into a living area for a tenant. He considered himself fortunate to be in such pleasant surroundings. Also, it wasn't far to walk to reach the bar around the corner where he was known to be a regular customer, and there was always someone there happy to have a conversation with him.

Frontius was content enough now, living where he was and

concentrating on his painting, especially the wall frescoes. With any luck, he'd be starting soon on the new one Calpurnius had described to him. He was never more contented than when he was working.

Few realised the extent of his talent and that was why he was so gratified to be commissioned to do work for Calpurnius Piso, who had the capacity to appreciate the quality of what he was seeing. Frontius was looking forward to painting the new fresco he'd mentioned that he wanted for his villa.

It wasn't fair that Livia had refused to pay him. It wasn't his fault that she'd left the colour choice to him. He'd have to think about whether to make an official complaint about non-payment if she didn't change her mind. He'd need as much money as he could save before he was too old to work any longer.

A few days elapsed following the altercation at the villa of Livia and Vennidius. Frontius decided to return there, which he did and knocked on the door. After a short wait it was opened by a servant who disappeared inside to ask if the master or mistress would see him.

Vennidius Ennychus came to the door and Frontius could see Livia standing back in the shadows behind him. Frontius was left standing in the doorway while Vennidius shouted at him for all the passers-by in the street to hear.

'No one asked you to paint the room black!' he roared. 'How dare you ask for payment.'

Frontius found himself embarrassed and unable to utter a word as Vennidius continued to rant and ramble on barely pausing for breath.

'And understand this, Frontius, I hope I make myself clear,' Vennidius continued, 'your fee will not be paid and that's that!'

The door was slammed in Frontius' face and he had no option but to leave. He returned to his apartment to think about the best way to handle the situation. The result was

Herculaneum: Paradise Lost

that he determined to find a way to do something about the incident in order to extract payment for the work he'd done.

Livia hated her life in Herculaneum.

She'd been happy enough when they'd lived in Rome. But no, that wasn't what her husband, Vennidius, wanted. He'd insisted that they move here because he'd visited the town once before, years ago. He'd fallen in love with its peace and quiet and location by the sea. In Rome, they'd lived in a lovely street on the Esquiline Hill. Livia liked the many festivals during the year and she enjoyed walking in the city's large parks or on the banks of the river.

Beside the sea wasn't really where she felt comfortable.

They had been blessed with a child, Vennidia, who sadly had died aged two years, but their lifestyle was pleasant enough living in one of the best houses in town where her few friends could come to visit her.

Livia, however, had never been so bored in all her life since settling in Herculaneum. She resented her husband for not giving more consideration to her wishes. A mean and sour woman by nature, she became even more so. Those who came to know her, were of the opinion that she created scenes just for a change from the utter boredom of her existence. Her husband was also disliked for his abrupt manner.

Needless to say, very few social invitations arrived at their door. If Livia ever received one, usually given to them due to the influence of their wealth, she sniffed, scowled and destroyed it. Most of the time, unless she happened to be in a particularly good mood, she made no effort to return an answer to the sender. She had other family members but they'd always lived in Rome.

'Are you home Livia?' Vennidius called as he stepped through the front door.

'Where else would I be?'

'At Florina's, perhaps?' Vennidius said, well aware that the lady mentioned was the only really close friend his wife had managed to find in the many years they'd lived there.

'No. As you can see, I'm not with her.'

Vennidius shrugged, not particularly surprised at his wife's tone. As he walked through the house, he suddenly stopped and gasped. 'What by all the gods is that?'

Livia joined him and was unsurprised to see his finger pointing towards the saloon with its black walls.

'Obviously, it's been painted,' she answered in an icy tone of voice.

'Surely, you didn't....'

There was an ominous pause.

'Please tell me you didn't ask for that colour!'

'Of course, I didn't!' Livia snapped.

'Then, why am I looking at it on the walls?' Vennidius retorted, his face like thunder.

Livia sighed with frustration. 'Frontius put it there.'

'He's obviously getting too old for this work,' Vennidius grunted. 'Have you paid him yet?'

'No! And I'm not going to.'

The House of the Stags
Cardo V

Livia decided that she needed to get out of her house, especially with Vennidius glowering and scowling every time he went anywhere near the saloon. She had no intention of putting up with it for the remainder of the afternoon, and decided that she would take herself off to visit Florina.

A short walk brought Livia to her friend's villa and with it came the usual feeling of jealousy that it aroused in her. Her own house did not in any way compare with the sophistication and elegance of the villa she was about to enter, despite Livia's house being located on the major street of the town.

The views of the sea that Florina enjoyed were stunning. All rooms except the atrium had been recently renovated, and enjoyed spectacular sea vistas. There was a pretty garden peristyle where graceful statues of stags and the god Hercules were strategically placed.

'Florina, it's Livia. Are you there?' she called upon reaching the atrium.

'I'm in the dining room,' a voice answered. 'Come through!'

This wasn't the first time that Livia had been further into Florina's villa but she never ceased to envy her the design and the furnishings she found there. She entered the covered walkway that linked the various interconnected rooms of the villa, staring inside each room as she slowly passed it. A multitude of magnificent wall frescoes decorated the whole house.

The two most captivating rooms were the large ballroom and the dining room. Livia found Florina standing studying the latter with a slight frown on her face.

She turned to greet Livia. 'It's good to see you. You'll stay to take some refreshments with me, I hope?' she smiled pleasantly. 'Everything needs to be perfect tonight. We have a few people, including one of the senators from Rome coming to dinner. I have to supervise everything or the servants just can't seem to get it right.'

Florina sighed.

'I'd love to.' Livia's mouth watered at the thought of the delectable small cakes her friend always served at such times.

'I have some news for you,' Livia began. 'You'll never guess what's happened at home. Vennidius is absolutely furious.'

'Really?'

She trailed Florina through to the garden.

The two women could not have been more unalike in just

about every way. How a friendship flourished between them amused everyone in town, however, it seemed to survive. Florina was as large as Livia was thin, and as happy and jovial as Livia was sour. No one could quite work it out, and they were often the topic of some nasty jokes.

'We'll take refreshments here in the garden,' Florina ordered the slave who came in response to the tinkle of her tiny silver bell. 'Be sure to include cakes,' she added.

Livia was about as contented as she ever became. She sat in the enchanting garden looking straight out at the sea as she enjoyed the delicacies Florina provided. Livia told her about the problems with the painting of the saloon, adding some embellishments.

Livia declared the morning tea, 'incredible.' She could have sat there much longer, but it became obvious that Florina was keen to return to her dinner preparations.

'Florina, if I promise not to disturb you, do you think I could sit up on your sun deck on the roof for a while?' she asked.

'Yes. That's not a problem,' Florina agreed pleasantly. 'It will be lovely and warm up there today. Now, I really must go and sort out this dining room problem. You'll be able to let yourself out, won't you?'

'Yes. Thanks, Florina.'

Livia watched her friend's retreating back then walked up the steps to the deck. She was not a lover of the seaside, but as she sat comfortably up there on a chair, she had a view of the other houses on the foreshore as well as of the beach. She found it interesting looking down into the other residents' adjacent gardens and watching people strolling on the beach below her.

A couple of children played near the water's edge. Their yells of delight reached her clearly where she sat. Sometimes, she missed her child who had died. Vennidia had been a sweet baby with curly black hair.

Next door, the neighbour had obviously received his

purchase of a large, new bronze urn. Livia watched as he fastidiously assessed its impact as it was placed at different angles on the marble stand on which it had been placed.

How interesting people were, she supposed. But they could also be intolerably boring and nasty. She decided that she was better off without most of them interfering in her life.

For a while Livia lay soaking up the sun.

By the time she left, her mood had improved considerably. She even had a slight smile on her face as she approached her front door. This did not happen very often, so Vennidius enquired as to where she'd been.

'I actually did go to see Florina,' she replied happily. 'We could have had a villa like that if we'd just remained in Rome. We could still move back again you know!' she added hopefully.

'You must be dreaming,' her husband replied gruffly. 'Do you have any idea how much that villa of hers cost to build?'

This was an old argument that would never be resolved in Livia's favour. The scowl returned to her face and turning her back on Vennidius, she retired to her bedroom in a huff.

The small patch of sunshine in her life had entirely disappeared.

6

BAIAE

North of Herculaneum

Emperors, consuls, senators and men of great wealth owned villas in this most prestigious of addresses outside Rome on the southern coast of Campania. As he entered the resort of Baiae, Calpurnius was overwhelmed, as he always had been, by the sheer beauty of the setting. A gentle breeze off the water relieved the heat. There was a dreamy languor about this place that drew any who entered into its spell.

A calm sea bordered by a pristine, sandy beach lay under an azure sky, its waves shimmering in the sunshine. Villas lined the steep clifftop and continued further inland from the water. Their owners lived in the utmost luxury in this peaceful paradise. Mosaic floored grottos, pools and private bathhouses were common-place.

Only the freshest of plump oysters and other seafoods and wine such as Falernian found their way onto dinner tables, and encircling volcanoes provided natural hot water and steam for baths and spas which were always in use.

Most of all, Baiae was a place of sensuality and seduction where any vice could be practised by both men and women. The nights, especially, were filled with sex, singing and sin of all kinds in settings of luxury unimaginable to other Romans.

Prostitutes, both young girls and boys were readily available. What happened in Baiae was not spoken about publicly.

Baiae was exclusive and wealthy, meant for only the highest of the elite. There was no other resort that compared. Some argued that Capri was just as exquisite, but most connoisseurs of such places grudgingly gave Baiae precedence.

The town sat in the giant crater of a huge volcano containing many small volcanoes within it, part of a large area named the fields of fire. The land was constantly gently rising and falling, as if breathing. The Romans happily made use of the thermal waters in their bathhouses with little knowledge or concern about the danger in which they placed themselves.

The Piso family had fallen into disgrace under the previous reign of the Emperor Nero, due to their part in an audacious conspiracy which had ultimately failed.

Although Calpurnius was from a different family branch, he felt the enormity of the disgrace greatly. At the time, the Piso family villa at the seaside luxury resort at Baiae had been confiscated, but it was then returned to the family by Vespasian when he came to power. Besides, it was not really the type of place that this emperor preferred.

'Calpurnius, you'll get far more use from the villa than I ever will! I'd be happy to see it in your hands,' the Emperor had told him. 'Take it with my blessing, it belongs back in your family.'

Vespasian was known to take his holidays each year in the countryside outside Rome, in the house of a friend of many years, who treated him as if he was simply an ordinary person and took no notice when Vespasian rambled through the countryside without protection, relishing the peaceful seclusion.

Vespasian's tastes were simple.

The Baiae villa formerly belonging to his family had become the property of Calpurnius.

It was even rumoured that the Piso villa was superior to the imperial villa that belonged to the Emperor. The wealth of the Piso family was on full display in this beautiful beachfront location.

The seafront estate had vast, immaculate gardens and its own fish breeding ponds as well as a private jetty. Exquisite frescoes filled the walls in colours of scarlet and expensive green and blues. The dining area included lighted wall niches in which stood priceless statues of water nymphs, and marble reclining areas lined its long, narrow pool. Food was floated along the water on tiny boats for diners to choose and enjoy.

It stood so close to the imperial residence it was said that before the conspiracy, Nero had often been seen walking on the clifftop between both villas without a bodyguard. Understandably, Gaius Piso, once the Emperor's close friend, was forced to commit suicide when his major role in the conspiracy became known.

Calpurnius determined that he would come here more often, even if only for short periods. He had almost forgotten how beneficial it was to spend time simply enjoying the life he had without the pressures of important decisions. This trip, however, was as much about business as pleasure, probably even more so.

'Welcome, Dominus!' he was greeted by one of the slaves responsible for ensuring that everything had been prepared for their master to enjoy.

'Salve! Is the villa ready for me?' Calpurnius asked.

'It has all been done, Dominus.'

Minutes after his arrival, he was standing on the villa balcony of his spacious bedroom looking out over the sea, as further down the beach, the oyster farmers worked their magic. The oyster shells hung from ropes attached to floating buoys in the water.

Slaves busied themselves quickly removing all signs of their presence, departing after leaving a large bowel of fruit on the table in the bedroom. The sun streamed in through balcony doors, lighting the precious floors underfoot. This was the domain of true wealth only the elite of Rome would ever experience.

The small town of Baiae catered to every whim of the rich. Ancient cyprus pines provided shaded resting places from the exhausting heat and pretty fountains were creatively placed at intervals to provide drinking water as well as to enhance the deception of coolness.

An expensive brothel, gambling establishment, clothing and jewellery stores, wine from Pompeii and overseas, all this and more could be bought here for enough money.

A considerable amount was won gambling, sometimes a fortune, but mostly lost on games such as dice. It was not totally unknown, even if rare, also, for wealthy men having consumed too much alcohol to bet even their villas in games of chance.

Coins were more easily coaxed from the purses of these wealthy holiday makers as they happily cavorted in the resort. Most, went home content.

Parties were common on boats sitting not far off-shore, many centring around naked or semi-naked young girls and boys. There were no rules except, perhaps, for murder. This, of course, covered accidents when someone fell overboard through intoxication.

Indulgence was encouraged. It was even celebrated.

It was on the fringes of the town, that Calpurnius had established his large statuary workshop. He employed only the most talented of sculptors he could find, and it was the known place for wealthy Romans to buy something special to show off in their gardens back in the city.

Copies of classical statues as well as marble busts and decorative garden urns were also available for purchase, but unknown to buyers, many of the Greek statues that they presumed were originals and for which they paid a fortune, were copies. But buyers went back to Rome ecstatic. The many sculptors who had continuing work were also happy and so were Calpurnius, Alexus and Vespasian.

'Salve, Stephanos!' Calpurnius greeted the workshop manager as he entered, refreshed after a deep sleep in the peace of his villa.

'It's good to see you, Calpurnius!' The manager strode over to greet him with a warm smile. 'Business is great,' he exclaimed enthusiastically.

'I had a feeling it might be from the grin on your face,' Calpurnius commented as they toured the workshop, stopping occasionally to speak to some of the sculptors and watching them create.

'Demetrius, do you enjoy your work as a sculptor?' Calpurnius questioned one of the artisans. 'Your skill is special and the statues you make or even just the copies, show great talent.'

The sculptor glanced across at him as he considered the question. 'Thank you, sir. This is always what I have done. I was trained as a young boy. My father did this work all his life and I have followed him. I know nothing else.'

Stephanos and Calpurnius nodded and moved on.

'There's a new original sculpture nearly finished which will arrive up here soon,' he explained to Stephanos. 'I'm also expecting others. Do you have enough sculptors to cope with copies of these as well as what we already have?'

Stephanos paused for a moment before replying. 'We could really do with one more artisan, but it may take me a while to find someone of the standard we're needing. Do you want me to start looking?'

'I'm sure you're right. Begin now and with any luck you'll have found someone by the time those statues get here. Take care, though, whoever he is, make sure you can trust him.'

'Yes, sir. I understand.'

Calpurnius stood watching as a small group of elderly men assessed the statues on display in the front garden, barely noticing him as they talked, they were so deep in discussion. It wasn't long before a couple of them liked what they saw and each bought one.

Unless Calpurnius was very wrong, Vespasian would certainly be pleased.

7

ROME

The Royal Palace
The Palatine

Vespasian sat quietly reflecting on the situation in which he found himself. It was only relatively recently that he'd contemplated any idea that he might become Emperor of Rome. Even then, the various factions vying for just that reward, had seemed too many and powerful for him to hope for anything other than retaining the position of the victorious general he already was.

Since then, his days had been caught up in a whirlwind of activity. Not that he'd ever misunderstood the many difficulties inherent in ruling an empire.

A man of simple needs, honest and decent, with a very ordinary country background, he was sometimes underestimated. Smart and resourceful, he understood much that was not always evident to those rulers who had gone before him.

He was a true emperor of the people.

Prior emperors had been busy constructing palaces and memorials to themselves, even whilst trying to keep ordinary citizens happy with their rations of bread and chariot races. When that system failed there were usually riots in the streets.

The victory arch at the Forum celebrating the conquest of Judea was just another memorial, Vespasian supposed, when he thought about it. The people, however, did still have their chariot racing in the Circus Maximus and gladiatorial combat to enjoy, the latter taking place in the Forum in a makeshift wooden stadium, limited in the number of people it could hold. It was erected when required and then dismantled. Gladiator combat was popular, but certainly overshadowed by chariot racing.

'This place is a dump! My bum hurts from trying to sit on these planks!'

A pleb's complaint floated across in a rare, less rowdy moment, to reach Vespasian's ears one afternoon. It was then that an idea came to him. He thought about it for a moment and then dismissed it, but found that his mind refused to release it.

He knew then, that he needed to give the people something else in the form of entertainment, something they'd never experienced before.

That had been six months ago.

Vespasian returned mentally to the present. He left the palace and walked slowly to the Gardens of Lucullus, shadowed at a distance by several praetorian guards. It was a glorious Roman day and for some time he wandered through the grounds, before sitting comfortably on a bench as he turned a variety of ideas over in his mind.

Afterwards, he simply enjoyed the warmth of the sunshine

on his face and the beauty of the surroundings. And yet, he wondered how a place could be this beautiful but also so deadly. He was fully aware of the executions and suicides that haunted the past of these lovely gardens. Both men and women had lost their lives in pursuit of their possession.

In reality, this place was soaked in blood.

Not for the first time, he considered the conundrum that Rome was a place of both light and shadow, of the greatness of men and the evil of which they were capable. The uncertainty he often felt was tempered, fortunately, by the faith he held in his son, Titus. Vespasian had no doubt that when the time came, he would make a great emperor.

Frowning, he finally rose and made his way to the site of his new endeavour. He gave a wry smile knowing that Nero would have been in a fury if he'd realised what his successor would do with the location of his magnificent Golden House.

Vespasian had already decided to build the Flavian Amphitheatre. Now, he had to turn the concept into reality.

'I require you only to follow me at a distance,' Vespasian ordered the shadowing praetorians. 'I intend to inspect the first foundations of the amphitheatre.'

As he neared the construction site of the great new project, he hoped that it would change Rome forever, and give the people something truly life-changing.

Vespasian's thoughts shifted to the gold being held in Herculaneum by Calpurnius Piso. He'd believed when he'd made that decision that it was safer with him than here in Rome. That was still the opinion he held, if only the secrecy surrounding the arrangement would just hold for a little longer.

'If there were more as loyal as Calpurnius,' he murmured to himself, 'there would be far less to worry about, but unfortunately, villains are a reality of this world.'

For a while Vespasian watched the gangs of bricklayers as they worked. They toiled hard in the hot sun, watched over by supervisors who were unrelenting in the pursuit of meeting their quotas for the day. Perspiration streamed from the slaves' bodies. Many of them came from Judea.

'Move! Move! We must win the day!' came the chanting from each team leader as the bricks were passed from hand to hand in long lines.

The slaves were divided into gangs, each of which had a name and they competed with one another to achieve the most bricks laid during every shift.

This helped to make their days more bearable. It also enhanced the deception of belonging to something greater than themselves.

8

POMPEII

Three years earlier

Prima was freeborn and came from a poor patrician family in the town of Nuceria, only twelve miles or so from Pompeii. Her family had lived in the area for many years and was well known. They could be described as poor patricians. The town was pleasant enough but as she left childhood behind, she knew that she couldn't stay there if she wanted a life better than that of her parents.

On an overcast day drizzling with light rain, she left Nuceria forever and with the help of an old friend and his creaking cart made her way to Pompeii, determined to make her fortune. At first sight, she was somewhat intimidated by the brashness and size of the city. Noisy and impersonal, it was the opposite of everything she'd been used to.

Near the busy harbour, she came to the well-located *Hotel of the Muses*. It was a structure decorated beautifully with works of art. Her mother, seeing that Prima wouldn't change her mind about leaving, had given her the largest number of coins she could possibly manage to spare. She hoped that her daughter would find work quickly.

Confused as to where she should go, Prima stepped inside the hotel. As soon as she did so, she realised her mistake. There was no way that she could afford this place with its splendid furnishings. She started to leave when the owner, who was standing beside the reception counter, approached her.

She was past her prime with dyed red hair and arms displaying many bangles that jangled when she moved. Somewhat overweight, her face was nonetheless, quite pretty and her voice soft.

'Welcome. I own this hotel. Are you looking for a room for the night?'

Embarrassed, Prima replied shyly, 'Yes, but I've made a mistake. There's no way I can afford your fine hotel.'

'Actually,' the owner informed her, 'this is a slow time of the year for us and we have a number of rooms vacant. You may stay here without paying for the night, if you're willing to serve dinner to the hotel guests. I'm short of staff at present. What do you think?'

'You're very kind. I'll gladly accept your offer.'

Prima couldn't believe her luck. Immediately, she was led to a room so luxurious that it left her gazing in wonder. Her duties serving meals that night were pleasant enough.

She'd never before slept in a bed so soft with such silky, fine linen as she did then. By the next morning when she left, she'd made up her mind that she wanted to be able to afford luxuries such as this.

But how was she to make such a dream come true?

One thing Prima did notice immediately on her arrival in Pompeii, was that she was constantly being stared at. She had long, fair hair, blue eyes and a voluptuous figure. The women ignored her and went on their way. It was the men who passed her on the street, or encountered her in a shop or anywhere else for that matter, who turned to look at her a second time. She found the attention confronting initially, until she became used to it as much as she was ever going to.

The problem she had, was that she was finding it difficult to obtain work and the small fund of money she had was beginning to diminish. She walked the streets from one end of the city to the other asking at a variety of shops and even grand villas, if there was any work for her, but there was none. She became tired and discouraged and her feet hurt.

'There's not much around at the moment, I'm sorry,' a good-natured inn keeper told her. Have you tried at the villa of the banker at the end of this street yet?'

'Thank you. I think so,' Prima replied. She was beginning to become disoriented she'd walked down so many streets until, finally, she sank down gratefully on to a bench in the garden of the Temple of Venus near the Marine Gate to rest.

A few days later, when walking towards the amphitheatre, she heard a woman's voice calling to her. A lewd comment had just been voiced towards her from a passing male. It had been loud enough for the woman and those nearby to hear.

'Lady, come over and join me. My name is Julia. I own this restaurant and bathhouse.'

At first, Prima hesitated. She was tired and somewhat dispirited, but she walked over to where the middle-aged woman stood beside the street food counter that was part of the large complex behind her.

'I don't know you. Are you new here?' the woman questioned her.

'Yes. I've only just arrived,' Prima answered.

'And where are you from?' Julia probed.

Herculaneum: Paradise Lost

'Nuceria.'

'Please, have a seat inside with me and rest. What's your name?'

'People call me Prima at home, but I don't know anyone here.'

'I'm Julia Felix. It seems to me that you could do with someone to talk to and a meal.' Without waiting for an answer, Julia ordered food for the girl from one of her staff.

'But, I can't pay for it,' Prima frowned.

'You leave that to me,' Julia smiled and patted the girl's arm. 'I own all of this complex and I'd like to help you. It's not safe for a young woman as beautiful as you are to wander alone in this city. The town you've come from is small and much quieter.'

They sat talking for some time during which Prima recounted the story of her background and what had brought her to Pompeii. There was something genuine and caring about Julia that encouraged Prima to trust her.

'I also provide lodgings here,' Julia told her when she'd heard Prima's story. 'I'd like you to stay in one of the rooms here where you'll be safe. If you wish to later, when you are earning properly you can pay me back.'

'I'm so grateful to you, Julia, but why would you do that for me?'

'Let's just say that I was young and not well off once. I know what it's like.'

Julia led Prima up the steps just behind the street food counter and showed her into one of the rooms. It was small but very clean, with a bed, chest of draws and flowers on top of a small desk. A window looked out onto Via dell'Abbondanza above the people passing by and allowed light into the room.

'Here, Prima, rest and if you wish, after dinner, we'll talk about what we might be able to do about your future.'

Julia left, closing the door behind her.

It had all been a little too much for Prima to cope with and she felt tears come to her eyes. She lay down on the bed and promptly fell asleep. She barely had time to get ready before it was dinner time. There was a soft knock on her door.

'Prima, it's Julia. Are you ready to eat?'

'Coming!' Prima called as she opened the door with some hesitation. She hoped that she was about to hear good news and whispered a quick prayer for luck to the goddess, Fortuna.

9

Together Julia and Prima went down the stairs to the pretty restaurant screened off from the main road by a well-kept hedge. The delectable smell of hot food reached Prima's nose and she realised that she was ravenously hungry. Once having ordered, the two women took up from where their last conversation had ended.

'Would you like to come with me to my bathhouse here in the morning?' Julia offered.

'Yes. That's kind of you,' Prima accepted.

'Have you had experience in any work before?'

'That's the problem, I haven't,' Prima acknowledged.

'Mmm.' Julia paused, thinking.

'I'll be truthful with you, Prima. There are really only three options open to you that I can see.'

Prima waited anxiously for her to continue.

'I'd be happy to train you to work on the fast food counter and after that, you could take orders and bring food to customers in the restaurant here. But I'm sorry to say that wouldn't pay very much, especially as you would have to allow enough money to give you somewhere to live.'

'And the other alternatives….?'

'You could get married. But that might take a while as you would need to meet some young men here first. It could also not be much of a choice because residents with money and good backgrounds, look for a girl from the same type of family to marry their sons.

The final possibility is one I hesitate to put forward, but the choice is yours. Men in Pompeii pay for favours from women who offer themselves within inns, outside bathhouses or even on the street. You're young and beautiful so you could command a high price. Give it a great deal of thought though, my dear, before you decide to choose that way of life. Once you do so, you can never go back.'

Prima was nearly in tears. Julia put her arm around her to comfort her.

'Have you ever *been* with a young man?' she asked softly.

'No.' Prima's reply was barely more than a whisper.

'I believe that you need a little time to think. Come, let us finish our dinner and a cup of wine might be a good idea.' Julia ordered it and no more was said about the problem until the next day.

Prima slept well.

She seemed preoccupied when Julia fetched her the following morning, but much calmer. After breakfast, they strolled through the lovely garden on Julia's estate to the bathhouse.

Entering, they undressed and entered the water. Julia kept the conversation light-hearted and they simply enjoyed the warmth and the relaxation that came naturally from soaking in peace in the perfumed water.

'This morning I'm going to take you to the Venus section

of the city,' Julia explained as they dressed. 'If you work as a prostitute from an inn or the city's brothels, some of what you earn will be kept by the owner. You may also need to place your name on a register but perhaps not, as you are freeborn. With your beauty and freshness, I believe that you can do much better than that.'

They left Julia's estate and as they walked further along the road, Prima saw women on the footpaths, some lounging against buildings, their hair dyed yellow.

'Are these the women you're talking about?' Prima asked with a frown as she studied them.

'Yes. But I'm hoping to achieve something a level up from that if you decide this is the life you want. I have to admit, there's good money to be made for the most seductive of the women. There are some very wealthy men in Pompeii.'

'Can you tell me where Lexia is?' Julia asked one of the street women.

'At her place, working,' she replied.

Lexia lived a short walk away over the narrow laneways. She came to the door at Julia's knock. She was happy to relate to Prima some of the details about what she did. She was better off than the street women as she had this poor but more private house from which to work, and she kept all of the money she earned herself.

'Goodbye, Prima,' she smiled as they parted. 'If you're desperate, come back to me here.'

As it turned out, Prima accidentally began her work in the oldest profession a few days later. One morning she was standing by the street food counter when she saw Julia talking to an older man at the entry to her bathhouse.

Julia gestured to her to join them. 'This is Sempronius Verus. He's asked to meet you.'

He smiled pleasantly at her. 'Julia has told me a little about you,' he began. He was well-dressed and courteous. 'I own an establishment called *The Gentlemen's Club*. I think you'd do well there as a lady of quality paid to satisfy the needs of our elite male clients. Would you like to come and have a look?' He paused to give her time to make her decision. 'If you wish,' he added, 'Julia can come with you.'

Prima glanced at Julia who nodded slightly to her.

'Thank you. I'd like to,' Prima answered hesitantly.

What she saw that day, and when she realised the money to be made from the wealthy members who belonged to the club, she had no reluctance in accepting Sempronius' offer. There were so few choices open to her and this was by far the best of them.

The club stood on Via di Nola. It was both exclusive and very private. Members enjoyed the very best of food, wine and surroundings. If they felt inclined to do so, they could even relax in the rear garden to the sound of water from a nympheum as gaudily coloured peacocks roamed past strutting and fanning out their eye-catching tails.

The clients Prima met and provided services for after she began working at the club considered themselves fortunate. It may be, that some of them even fell a little in love with her.

Sempronius provided for her use a beautifully decorated bedroom which also had the only private bathing facility at the club. It was located at the rear of the building with windows looking out over a private garden. As soon as he'd first met her, he'd recognised the likelihood of success that Prima began to enjoy very soon after she began working there.

Most of the men were the very wealthy of the city. They not only paid her but she was often given gifts as well. They conversed with her about their families, their businesses and told her their secrets. Prima's reputation for discretion and beauty spread, so it was no surprise that she was also approached by some rich gentlemen who lived in nearby Herculaneum. She was in the fortunate position of being able to take a great amount of care choosing the clients she agreed to service.

Within three years, Prima became the most elite and wealthy courtesan in Pompeii and Herculaneum. Her activities were much more pleasant than she'd anticipated, due largely to the environment in which she worked, and she found some of the secret information her clients shared with her both interesting and sometimes, surprising.

It wasn't long before Prima had saved enough to afford a small house, not in the wealthy part of Pompeii, but at least in an area that was safe and attractive. She bought a property not far from the residence of the surgeon. They exchanged greetings as she walked past on most days, and soon began to converse more.

Before long, Prima had made new friends and she insisted on repaying Julia Felix for the money she'd spent on her. The two women remained firm friends, meeting up on a regular basis to discuss their joys and troubles.

Prima was popular and had the financial security that she'd longed for. An added benefit was that she controlled her own life. The owner and staff of *The Gentlemen's Club* became her surrogate family.

10

HERCULANEUM

House of the Hotel (Albergo)
Insula III

79 A.D.

Prima smiled broadly as she alighted from the carriage that had transported her the short distance from Pompeii. The hotel's owner, Cassia, hurried out to meet her, pleased to greet the guest who had made reservations for three days of every week for the immediate future. She knew the woman was a courtesan but was unaffected by that. If Prima was a quiet guest who did not ply her trade within this, the only luxury hotel in Herculaneum, then Cassia really didn't care.

'Salve, Prima,' she smiled in greeting.

'Salve, Cassia, I'm so pleased to be here,' Prima responded courteously.

She was led into the hotel and taken to the guest services desk where she duly gave her name and replied when asked, that she would, indeed, appreciate a daily breakfast during her stay. She looked around assessing her surroundings, as she had often been in Herculaneum before, but never in this hotel.

The hotel was large with two peristyles, one with lemon and olive trees and the other, a sunken garden. Water tinkled from a central garden fountain and the air was fragranced with perfume from oleanders, narcissus, violets, iris, roses, hyacinth and more. Box hedges added a more formal touch.

There were two entries. The main one, larger than the other, led into the reception area with comfortable couches, lamps and a floor resplendent with inlaid marble.

Generous arrangements of fresh flowers decorated desks and tables and outside, the sun deck proved to be a popular area with guests who sought warmth and relaxation. The view of the sea was an added spectacular attraction.

The hotel was everything any discerning guest could desire. It was popular with visitors throughout all seasons and was rarely left with vacant bedrooms.

'What a delightful place!' Prima exclaimed as one of the servants took her belongings to the allocated room to which Cassia also accompanied her.

'If there is anything you need just ring the bell,' Cassia advised Prima when she'd been shown into the suite. 'As you can see, this particular room has its own bath and opens out into a small private garden where you can sit if you wish.'

Prima smiled her thanks.

The room was light and well furnished. This would do nicely, she decided. As she lay down on the bed to rest before lunch, she was pleased and very happy with the arrangements made for her. Coming for short periods of time to Herculaneum each week instead of living permanently in Pompeii could prove to be a very good idea.

Prima already had plenty of work in Herculaneum. It suited her, though, to have less travel and disruption and her change of schedule might also help her clients to see her more often, if she spent several days each week in the town.

On leaving Prima's room, Cassia sat on one of the couches in the hotel reception room waiting for the next guest to arrive. Thoughtfully, she assessed her latest arrival. The young woman had true, natural beauty and seemed not only pleasant, but also intelligent. Cassia had watched as her glance had quickly, but carefully, taken in her surroundings. Cassia concluded that she'd like to get to know Prima better.

That afternoon, Prima set out to keep her appointment by the sea at the new, elegant suburban baths with Hermeros, a harmless, middle-aged banker from Puteoli who'd been one of her regular clients for some time. He'd been attempting lately to persuade her to visit him at his estate in Puteoli, north of Herculaneum, but she had laughingly pleaded lack of time and not taken up his offer due, she said, to her busy schedule.

Prima was amused when she got to the baths to see that yet another scribble had been added to the outside of the bathhouse wall:

Hermeros to Primigenia conqueror of hearts, greetings!

This message and many cheerful others, were apparently written by clients as they waited for her. She was immensely popular. She was also the keeper of many secrets, but the men who told them to her were never anxious from worrying that she'd ever repeat them.

Prima was regarded as a trusted confidante.

The bathhouse gleamed with marble. It had been built as a place of luxury.

Time has erased what happened during her rendezvous with Hermeros that day, but Prima would have been well paid for her company.

House of the Hotel (Albergo)
The next morning

Cassia's eyes widened in alarm when she saw the broken tesserae of the intricate black and white mosaic beneath her feet. How had it happened? She checked the other vacant rooms then walked out onto the sundeck which had a spectacular view towards the bay. Everything else seemed to be undamaged as far as she could tell. And then her vision swam as she caught sight of the new wall fresco in the main reception room. Someone had deliberately attacked part it with some sort of implement.

'Are you all right?' the housekeeper, Marilla asked as she approached Cassia from the portico. Her employer began to sway from side to side.

'You look ill. Can I get you something?' Her question was answered for her as she caught sight of the damage to the fresco. For a few moments both women said nothing, simply gazing at the wall in disbelief.

'Come, Cassia,' Marilla said firmly, taking her arm, 'sit down and I'll get you a cup of wine.' Cassia did as she was ordered and sank into a comfortable couch in the reception room.

'There's also damage to one of our expensive mosaic floors,' she told Marilla as she returned and handed her the cup. 'I can't even begin to think which guest could have done it. This is devastating!'

Marilla sat down beside her, silent for a moment or two. 'I'm not totally convinced that it was a guest,' she said thoughtfully. 'Perhaps someone from outside has done this. I realise that we know most of the guests. They come here year after year. I'm also aware, though, that there are always some who are unknown to us, even though, not many. Perhaps, indeed, it was one of them.'

Frontius was drifting in and out of a soothing dream when there was a knock, more like a loud banging, on the door to his apartment. He opened the door cautiously to find one of the assistants from the hotel standing there looking agitated.

'Frontius there are problems at the hotel. Cassia sent me to ask you to come urgently and she'll explain why when you get there.'

'Give me a few minutes and I'll join you,' Frontius grimaced as he closed the door and quickly pulled out a tunic and sandals. Together, they walked briskly down the road and saw Cassia waiting for them in the hotel portico.

'Thank you for coming, Frontius. We have damage to the fresco that you painted for me and I'd like you to look at it. Please come through.'

Frontius did so.

'Can you repair it?' she asked, concerned, as they stood studying the wall fresco.

'I believe so,' Frontius reassured her. 'I can find time late tomorrow to do it. I realise with guests here, this is urgent.'

Cassia nodded gratefully at him. 'That's a relief,' she sighed. 'Now the question of the floor mosaic.'

Frontius frowned as he examined it carefully. He shook his head.

'You need someone who has real skill with mosaics to repair this. Leave the problem with me and I'll see if I know anyone who can do it.'

Cassia's eyes filled with tears. Turning to Frontius she simply asked, 'Why?' She shook her head.

'Do you have enemies, perhaps someone you've recently argued with?'

'I don't think so,' she answered, searching her memory.

'Try not to worry. Everything will be fixed, but it might be an idea to have someone on duty at night to supervise entry through the main entrance. Close and lock the other entry. I wouldn't be surprised if this was done by someone with a grudge or more likely just some stranger from outside. You also might want to check that nothing is missing. I'm sorry but I really must go.'

Frontius liked Cassia. She was gracious to everyone and he was sorry to see her so upset. Perhaps he'd mention it to someone who might have the power to look into the problem.

Prima had slept late and awoke when all of the chaos was over. Nonetheless, she also felt sorry for Cassia and did her best to comfort her.

The Basilica
VII.16

Herculaneum's Basilica was rectangular, huge and divided laterally by two rows of central columns. Porticoes were enclosed by outer walls. Statues stood in niches along the inner walls and at the far end stood a lifesize statue of the Emperor, Vespasian. It was the central feature of a semi-circular recessed area. Either side of the central statue were enhanced with statues and frescoes depicting Chiron and Hercules.

The interior of the Basilica was also decorated with other precious frescoes and at its entrance stood a bronze, four horse chariot. Marble decoration adorned the doorway.

A noisy auction of slaves was taking place in the portico of the building on this morning. Most of the slaves on offer had originally been loaded onto a boat at the Greek island of Delos, a major slave trading centre. Scruffy, naked and underfed, they were dragged one by one onto the portico and the owner came forward to point out their attributes to potential buyers.

'This man is older than the others, but do not judge him only by his age. He is a Greek scholar and can provide your children with a good education as a tutor!'

The old man, dignified, with a grey beard, stood stoically staring straight ahead of him as the bidding progressed. He was eventually sold to a wealthy resident with a family of young children.

The senior magistrate, Aquilius Publicus, had an office in the Basilica. He was an efficient, gruff but decent man, elected because although he wasn't all that well liked, more due to the duties he had to perform than from personal dislike, he certainly got things done. As Frontius entered his office, Aquilius, formally dressed in his toga, gestured to him to be seated.

'It seems that you wish to discuss a problem pertaining to law and order with me. Is that correct?' he began.

'It is, sir. As the lady who suffered from the crime has no husband, I felt that I should attempt to gain justice for her.'

'An honourable sentiment. Now, tell me what has happened?' Aquilius' face grew more and more grave as the story of the incident at the hotel unfolded. 'I've been in that hotel myself,' he commented. 'It's a place of great beauty and refinement. If Cassia is the lady in charge that I vaguely remember, then she is a woman of courtesy with a pleasant disposition.'

'Yes, I find her so, sir.'

'Is the lady missing any other items?'

'I believe she is missing some valuable pearls that once belonged to her mother,' Frontius explained.

'Leave the problem with me. I'm interested not only in the damage done and the theft of the pearls, but also in the emotional trauma that the hotel owner has undoubtedly suffered. I'll solve this crime if I possibly can. I don't like the idea of property owned by defenceless women, causing them to be preyed upon, is stolen or damaged.'

Aquilius stood, indicating that the interview was over.

'Thank you, sir.'

'Salve. It's a credit to you. You've done your public duty. Is there anything else you wish to discuss with me?'

'Actually, sir, there is.'

Calmly, the magistrate waved the court officers away and proceeded to sit down again.

Frontius described the dispute he was having with Livia and Vennidius over the black walls of the saloon in their house and the non-payment of his fee, as well as how abusive they'd been. Their shouting had been overheard even in the street, which could damage his professional reputation.

'Assure me of one thing,' Aquilius interrupted him. 'Livia did say that she'd leave the choice of colour to you. Do I have that correct?'

'Yes. That was very clear.'

Aquilius stood once more.

Frontius murmured his thanks and left. He wasn't sure that he'd ever hear anything more about either of the two matters, but he knew that he owed it to himself and Cassia to at least try. He felt that he didn't deserve to lose money because of Livia any more than Cassia deserved to have her hotel damaged.

One thing Frontius didn't know, was that Aquilius and Vennidius, an ex-slave, disliked one another intensely. The magistrate considered him to be a lazy, no-good minor criminal. Aquilius' decision had already just about been made before he even further considered the evidence.

That afternoon Frontius returned to Cassia's hotel where he repaired the wall fresco. It took him longer than expected due to the position of the knife slashes, especially to the face of the goddess in the fresco. It was delicate work and very exacting. Fortunately, when he'd finished, it was difficult to see where the damage had occurred. If nothing else, no one could ever say that he wasn't a perfectionist with his paintings.

Frontius took with him a mosaic artisan who was an acquaintance. The floor damage proved to be a real problem. It was deep and irregular and it took hours for the artisan to fix it and make it secure.

'I'm sorry,' he told Cassia. 'I've done my best with this, but it will never be quite the same as before. Still, it should last you for a few years.'

The two men had stopped at the top of the street before arriving and discussed just how much of a fee reduction they could give Cassia in order to help her financially. Both agreed on very low rates in an effort to assist her.

She was very grateful, offering them a meal before they left and smiling her thanks at them. She vowed after they'd gone that she'd visit the temple of Isis not far from the hotel, from time to time, to give thanks for the kindness of those around her.

'I feel quite refreshed,' one of Cassia's frequent guests smiled at her later that day as she prepared to leave the hotel. 'This town really is a tiny piece of paradise!'

Cassia stood waving as the woman's carriage departed. The sentiment caused her to stop and think. It crossed her mind that it was time she appreciated what she had and how fortunate she was.

As for Frontius, he opened his apartment door several days later to find a messenger standing there. The man handed him a bag of coins.

'This is for you with compliments from the senior magistrate, Aquilius Publicus,' he said.

'Thank you!' Frontius answered and his face creased into a delighted grin.

Quickly, he shut the door and threw the bag on the top of his bed. Then, he ran over and emptied it. The contents fell out in a shower of gold.

He counted the coins. It was the exact sum of money owed to Frontius from Livia and Vennidius for his painting fee.

Or was it?

He counted them again carefully. A few extra had been added, probably to cover a penalty for late payment.

Frontius couldn't believe his good fortune. The magistrate had kept his promise. He immediately sat down to write a message of thanks to magistrate Aquilius Publicus.

The messenger approached the court officer standing in front of the door of the magistrate's office. The boy held up the message so that he could see it.

'I have a delivery for magistrate Publicus!'

'He's busy. He has no time to see anyone else today but give it to me and I'll hand it to him later.'

'As you like,' the boy replied, gave it to him and left.

The court officer returned to his own work until, by the time the afternoon was nearly finished, he'd almost forgotten the message.

Eventually, Aquilius finished for the day and opened his door. It was handed to him.

'Thank you. I'll remember this man's name,' he declared after he'd scanned the contents. 'In all my years as a magistrate, only three or four people over that time have made the effort to write their thanks when I've helped them.'

He took Frontius' message with him and placed it at home on his study desk. He could see it easily there at a glance.

It made him feel good.

Part II

Fools' Gold

11

ROME

PORTUS
(The Port of Rome)

A distinctive lighthouse resembling that at Alexandria stood magnificently signalling the entry to Rome's huge new port complex. The similarity was undoubtedly no accident. This one if measured, however, would probably have been found to be slightly taller.

Rome would never be outdone!

The port with its lighthouse solved the problem of Rome's dependence on the ancient, silted-up anchorage at Ostia. It also provided huge bays forty feet high for housing vessels in need of repair as well as every other facility imaginable.

Through this new harbour built by Claudius, came wealth arriving in the form of slaves, grain, and commercial goods.

Most of all, gold and treasures destined for the Emperor Vespasian's treasury passed through the port destined for Rome.

The harbour-master, Quintus Ampliatus, middle-aged and experienced in his work, took each day as it came, earning a decent living while residing in the small villa to which he was entitled on the fringe of the huge complex.

His young friend, Atticus, had worked with him for several years.

One cold and desolate night Quintus sat hunched over his desk in a small room of the warehouse adjacent to the harbour. The room was poorly lit by several oil lamps, the pool of light they emitted, insufficient for easy reading. Rubbing the tiredness from his eyes and standing to stretch his aching back, Quintus glanced out of the window into the blackness beyond.

Something near the dark waters of the harbour mouth caught his attention. It was a pinprick of light that flickered on and off a second time then there was nothing. Quintus decided to finish and go home. When he left his office everything seemed normal, but that night he couldn't stop thinking about the light he was sure he'd seen.

There was nothing adjacent to the port except the island of death. It was a place best forgotten.

The Sacred Island was an island of the dead.

The stench of death was everywhere. An angry sea pounded relentlessly against the shoreline and stinking marshes with their putrid odour of vegetation and sucking reeds made safe walking difficult.

Expensive mausoleums stood side by side further inland with simple, ancient headstones some of which lurched drunkenly to one side, victims of the relentless passing of time. After dark the island was thought to be haunted by evil spirits. On nights when the wind howled, it was said to be the screaming of ghosts.

Souls residing on *The Sacred Island* would never leave this place of mourning. It was here that Quintus brought Atticus the next morning.

'This is where I saw the flickering light,' Quintus explained.

'It's easy to imagine things after dark, as you know,' Atticus answered hesitantly. 'Are you sure?'

'Absolutely sure.'

'But no one ever comes here except for an occasional funeral and that's never at night.'

'That's why we should have a closer look,' Quintus insisted. He walked towards where the damp sand had been disturbed leaving the imprint of indentations made by footprints and other activity on the wet sand. Soon, they would disappear as the water level changed once more.

'I knew it!' he shouted to Atticus over the noise of the wind. 'There's very recently been a boat of some kind here, possibly loading something. Come and look!'

Atticus peered down at the marks on the damp sand. 'It's certainly possible,' he agreed.

A glint from something shiny caught his eye as it shone in the early morning sunlight. He began to search around the reeds where they met the sand. Quintus joined him and together they went down on their knees probing and pulling at the reeds.

'Well, here we have proof,' Quintus exclaimed triumphantly. His fingers felt and then withdrew two shiny gold coins from where they'd fallen into a tangle of reeds. They bore the imprint of Vespasian.

'I don't know what it is, but something's going on, all we have to do is find out what. And why are these coins here?' he questioned aloud. 'Obviously, they're new. They haven't even been here long enough yet to be totally covered by sand.'

From that moment, Quintus and Atticus hid on the island each night watching for any sign of activity. It was bone chillingly cold and damp but still they waited.

Marcus, centurion in charge of transferring Vespasian's chests of gold to Calpurnius in Herculaneum, was feeling uneasy. He couldn't quite work out why, but something he'd either seen or heard had triggered a subconscious alarm. His intuition told him that something was wrong. He was a careful man and diligent in his duty, which explained his selection for the important task of transferring the gold.

A few days after the most recent transaction, he sat thinking in his room in the guard barracks when he heard a knock at the door. He made no effort to get up and open it.

'Intrare,' he muttered distractedly.

'Are you going to sit there thinking all night?' his best friend, Octavius, asked as he stuck his head round the door. 'You can't see a thing with the lamp off. What are you doing sitting in the dark?'

In an instant Marcus realised the answer to the problem he'd been wrestling with.

'You're a genius!' he exclaimed, startling a surprised Octavius into silence.

On the night of the last gold transfer the whole of the port had been dark including the island, except for one tiny light coming from a building in or near one of the warehouses. And that light had been directly opposite where they were leaving the island bound for Herculaneum, having loaded chests of gold onto the boat. Marcus' mind had paid it no attention because it was just a solitary twinkle of light in the distance.

He needed to find out who had been over there and observed his own light, possibly from a flare. How much did they know? He also had to alert Vespasian, even if the chance of anything being amiss was probably very small.

The Palatine Hill
The Royal Palace

Marcus had always felt comfortable in the city of Rome. He seldom spent much time there, being usually on overseas postings.

Entering on horseback, he rode slowly through the throngs of people and onwards until he reached the Palatine Hill. Recognised, but challenged none the less by the guards on sentry duty, once inside he made his way to the reception area where he gave his name and asked for a meeting with Vespasian or his son Titus.

'Salve, Marcus,' Titus greeted him when he entered the tablinum. 'Father's over at the amphitheatre. I've told him he could save himself a great deal of time if he just slept there!' he laughed. 'I trust you're well?'

'Yes, thank you, sir. I don't wish to waste your time, but I must report something that may be totally unnecessary, or perhaps, of the utmost urgency.'

Marcus saw that he had Titus' full attention. He recounted his thoughts concerning the gold consignments to Herculaneum from the loading base at Portus, then sat silently waiting for Titus' reaction.

'As you well know, Marcus, I'm a soldier myself. I've learned over the years never to neglect to check out what I'd call a "gut" feeling, especially when it comes from a military man. Leave this with me. I'll need to discuss it with the Emperor but I'll be very surprised if he doesn't want to follow up on this.'

'Yes, sir.'

'And, Marcus, even if this turns out to be of no importance, thank you for your diligence. We'll be in touch with you. Salve.'

'Thank you, sir. Salve.'

Marcus felt a weight lifted off his shoulders as he left the palace. This was now the problem of others well above his power of authority.

Titus wasted little time before hurrying over to the amphitheatre where he found Vespasian chatting to one of the work gang supervisors.

'What brings you here?' Vespasian asked, relaxed and pleased with the progress of the construction. 'I thought you were concentrating on administrative work today.'

The problem that Marcus had just left him with was explained in detail by Titus. His father frowned in concentration and quickly made a decision.

'Something must be done and urgently. I don't think this is any coincidence. My suggestion is that we set a trap. See what you can think of that will not arouse the suspicions of these men, but we'd better move fast or the gold will be at risk. By Jupiter! I need every coin of it if the amphitheatre is to be finished!' His hands were tightly clenched.

Titus agreed and walked quickly back to the palace. There he sat thinking for some time until, finally, he gave a satisfied smirk. He'd worked out how to put a plan in place to foil what would almost certainly be an attempted robbery.

A message sent by Titus was sent to Calpurnius' villa in Herculaneum appraising him of the situation. One was also despatched to Marcus together with further, specific instructions. A third message was then relayed to a secret destination.

Herculaneum: Paradise Lost

In Herculaneum, Calpurnius arrived back home from Baiae several days later and was given Titus' message immediately. He frowned as he sat down to re-read it. He'd dreaded the possibility that the secret of the gold would be discovered. Now, his worst fears seemed to have been realised.

Tired and alarmed, he knew he had to trust in the probability that Titus had enough resources to deal with the plotters before their plans were too far advanced. He was an organised and efficient army man with huge means at his disposal. There wasn't really anything that Calpurnius could do himself.

He obviously couldn't guard the door where the gold was held all day and night. Even if he did, physically, he didn't have the resources to prevent an intrusion. In fact, it could become a very dangerous situation.

He walked slowly through the villa and came upon a sight that restored his spirits. Standing in the centre of the reception room was one of the most seductive and alluring statues he'd ever seen. Decius and Helena had finished, and it stood there in all its solitary glory.

For a few moments Calpurnius' stood fixed to the spot, his eyes drawn to the statue like a magnate. Then his morale lifted and a smile spread slowly across his face. Everything would surely work out well in the end. All he needed was patience and to remain as alert as possible. He retired to his room to sleep and awoke after ten hours refreshed and mentally sharp.

Calpurnius accepted that he couldn't either predict or probably alter the future, no matter what it was. His best efforts would have to be enough.

12

Nero's Golden House

'The man was obviously insane!' Vespasian exclaimed as he stood with his son, Titus, amidst the remains of one of the most luxurious areas of Nero's Golden House. Torrents of water cascaded down the full length of a very high wall before splashing forcefully into a pond at the bottom. Spray flew from it like small baubles of silver and the sound of the water crashing down from so high above, reverberated around the huge room. He studied the interior of the cavernous space in disbelief. Titus had the same stunned expression on his face. Vespasian's look of amazement turned to anger when rose petals began to fall on them from above.

'I can understand luxurious living, but this is absolutely ridiculous, not to mention wasteful,' Vespasian commented critically, 'I'm surprised Rome's people weren't in open revolt against Nero long before his suicide.

And turn off those rose petals immediately!' he spluttered angrily.

Glorious wall frescoes and gilded pillars still looked back at them, but their days were nearly over. It wouldn't be long before only empty spaces and a shadow of the Golden House's former glory remained.

Nero's large lake had already been drained, however, the towering statue of him as Sol, the sun god, remained intact, at least for now.

Adjacent to where they were standing, the noise, dust and chaos of the amphitheatre building site continued. The raw framework of much of the structure was close to completion. Eventually, statues would be brought in to fill the niches and interior and painters would arrive to decorate and beautify it.

Rome's citizens gaped in astonishment as the full impact of the amphitheatre became apparent. Some approached the site so that they could stand and watch in disbelief.

And that was just at the activity that could be easily seen, which did not include the mechanisms underneath the floor of the stadium.

The royal box and the nearby area reserved for archers, should additional security be needed, were not yet in place, but the final stages of construction loomed closer now.

'Are you sure that Marcus understands his instructions about the delivery of the next gold shipment?' Vespasian questioned his son. 'It won't be long before we need the extra coins from Herculaneum to finish the amphitheatre. The Treasury is running quite low.'

'Everything is ready,' Titus reassured his father. 'The plan will unfold in just a few nights and we'll see if the scum planning the robbery take the bait. I've also put in place other precautions that you needn't concern yourself with.'

Satisfied, Vespasian turned away to watch a large foundation stone nearby that was presently being carved with his name. It would be laid in place at the opening of the amphitheatre. For a while he stood silently observing it with satisfaction until his name was finally complete.

Vespasian felt a surge of pride and fulfilment. In comparison with the amphitheatre itself, this seemed a small accomplishment, but, in reality, it was representative of the whole achievement. The name of the Flavian dynasty would never be erased.

PORTUS
The Sacred Island

Quintus and Atticus found it was easier to wait for further activity on the *Island of Death* if they took turns watching at night. At least, that way, one of them could hope for a night's sleep. Quintus secretly had begun to wonder if they'd been wrong about the gold coins they'd found and the marks in the sand.

He was half dozing, trying to forget how cold he was one night, sitting not far from the shoreline, when he heard the unmistakable sound of voices. Suddenly alert, he listened intently. From what he could hear there seemed to be a small group of men approaching the spot where he'd found the gold coins, and also a boat or maybe even two being pulled up onto the bank.

It was dark and difficult to make out anything but hazy shapes. What Quintus did not see, were two of the legionaries creeping away in the opposite direction and hiding amongst the reeds not far from him. He thought he could just make out chests being unloaded from one boat and placed into another, much larger in size.

'Be careful. Don't drop any of them!' a voice of authority

barked an order. 'This is the last delivery to Herculaneum and then our job is done, but stay alert. We'll hit rougher waves once we leave here.'

The words carried clearly on the still night air. It never occurred to Quintus that perhaps that was no accident.

The first, smaller river boat, eventually turned and retreated back in the direction it had come, from Rome. The second, a large ocean-going vessel, originally innocently anchored in the Portus harbour, but now holding the gold chests, re-entered the water and disappeared further south towards Herculaneum.

As soon as it had gone, Quintus came out of hiding but had barely walked several paces before he felt himself restrained by strong arms and a gladius being held at his throat.

The next morning, Atticus searched in vain for Quintus who was nowhere to be found. He became more and more frantic as time went by and almost incapable of making a decision about what to do. Finally, word reached him in the form of gossip that Quintus had been arrested and was presently being interrogated in Rome. It was something apparently, to do with an issue that no one knew anything about.

Atticus began to panic. He fled from Portus. As long as Quintus kept his mouth shut, though, he was relatively sure that no one would know that he'd also been involved.

He decided to go south to Herculaneum, just in case Quintus was released and their plans went ahead. It wasn't very likely, but Atticus felt he had nothing to lose and staying in Portus was simply asking for trouble.

It was far too close to Rome for comfort!

The Palatine Hill
The Royal Palace

Quintus was smart enough not to resist.

Guards marched him in the dead of night up the Palatine Hill to the palace. He shook with fear.

'What are you going to do with me?' he asked, his voice barely above a whisper.

Silence.

They entered through a small door at the very back of the palace, and he was dragged down several flights of stairs to the basement. The door was slammed shut.

Quintus spent a night he'd rather forget in the bare, uncomfortable cell, his mind spinning with thoughts of torture or execution because of what he'd conspired to do. The first pale shades of morning glimpsed through the one high cell window, brought the return of the guards.

Given a cup of weak wine to drink, he spluttered as he tried to swallow it, then his captors retreated with him back up the stairs and into the back of the palace. They hadn't gone far when they entered a small, barely furnished room where he was pushed into a chair.

It seemed like an eternity that he sat there waiting, for what, he didn't know. His trembling increased and he kept twisting his finger ring around nervously, unable to stop himself from doing so.

Momentarily, he closed his eyes as he saw Titus, brother of the Emperor, stride purposefully into the room. He studied Quintus as a spider might observe a fly. Then, he sat and the interrogation began.

'Where is your accomplice?' Titus asked bluntly.

'I was on my own,' Quintus squeaked.

'So, you were working alone, were you?' He persisted with the same line of questioning for some time, but Quintus refused to change his story.

'I've told you! I was on my own and I was just walking on the island to get some fresh air,' Quintus insisted, attempting unsuccessfully to stop his voice from faltering.

'Your story isn't convincing. If I were you, I'd take this as a severe warning,' Titus declared sternly. 'I don't believe you. That's a strange place to choose for a pleasant night's stroll, but you weren't caught in the act of a crime and you also weren't carrying a weapon, therefore, I'm inclined to show some leniency here.'

Quintus looked hopeful for the first time. He made an attempt to keep his hands still.

'That being the case,' Titus continued after a short pause, 'I will order your release on this occasion. You may leave, but stay out of trouble!'

'Thank you, sir!'

The guards stood aside and Quintus virtually ran out the door, down the passageways and out of the palace. He failed to see the slight nod that Titus gave to another man of nondescript appearance, standing silently observing at the back of the room.

From now on, Quintus would be under permanent surveillance by one of the praetorian guard's best undercover agents. The odds of being the victor in this contest were definitely not on his side.

The agent, by the name of Cletus, followed his target effortlessly staying at all times in sight of him, but not risking discovery. Unaware of his true situation when he returned to Portus, Quintus was handed a message that Atticus had left for him.

I will be in Herculaneum staying at the inn near the silversmith's shop. I'll wait there for as long as I can. I've made no plans yet beyond that.

Quintus rode as quickly as he could for Herculaneum. If he was in time, there was at least some chance that he and Atticus could at last find exactly where the gold was being hidden and decide what to do from there. This was the opportunity of a lifetime and he had in intention of letting it go to waste.

Cletus wasn't someone who'd be noticed, not at this very moment, anyway. That was not by accident, as it was necessary for him in his role to be able to blend in with his surroundings. Highly trained and very experienced, he knew his job and did it well. Intelligent and innovative, he'd been noticed early in his army career and recruited to Vespasian's undercover force. A soldier's physique was hidden under rags. He was deadly with a gladius.

Cletus was dressed in the clothes of a beggar, his hair was long and matted and his face unwashed, but he rode like the expert horseman he really was. Having been given the facts of Quintus' case, he knew that he was surely heading for Herculaneum. Nonetheless, Cletus decided he would still shadow Quintus, unobserved, at least as far as the city walls.

And that's exactly what he did.

13

HERCULANEUM

An Inn
Just inside the town walls

A tiny inn just inside the town gate stood, or rather, leaned, against the inner side of the wall. Few ever noticed it as they passed through the busy gate. It had just three guest bedrooms and a tiny reception room and was gravely in need of a multitude of minor repairs. Nonetheless, despite the garden surrounding it, once colourful but now overgrown and uncared for, there remained an echo of the pretty establishment it had once been.

There was nothing pretty, however, about the thoughts of the man who lay depressed on the bed in one of the rooms. Poorly dressed and with nothing much to his name other than the stained tunic he wore, he'd reached the point where he was desperate for enough money to pay for his lodging, food and wine.

His name was Spurius.

He got up and paced up and down the small room.

Suddenly he grinned as a plan came to him. 'I think I know what the answer is,' he spoke aloud, pleased with himself. 'I need to go somewhere else!'

Spurius sat down, lost in thought.

'I know just the place. It's wealthy, I've never been there before, but from what I've heard Pompeii is certainly big enough for me to keep out of sight and hopefully, out of trouble.'

Spurius reflected further on his situation. He wouldn't have needed to put his plan into action if that woman, Cassia, at the hotel, hadn't taken his job away just because he was accused of being rude to one of the women staying there. He'd been earning enough working at the hotel to be able to pay for his basic needs, especially as he was allowed to eat a free dinner each night when he finished his duties.

But, without warning, he'd been tossed out like a piece of rubbish.

The knife he'd stolen afterwards had felt good in his hand, when he'd entered the smaller door into the hotel through the garden one night after dark.

He rubbed his hands together with glee. He'd already made her pay. It would cost her a small fortune to fix that fancy mosaic and the damaged wall fresco. He wondered if she'd discovered the missing pearls yet that he'd stolen from the chest in her room. Spurius had rather liked the feeling of them in his hands. They felt clean and cool, but he knew he couldn't keep them, which was a pity.

He'd sold them immediately to one of the dealers in the town for a good price. That would be enough, he reasoned, to pay ahead for his rent and buy food. First, he'd have a few days rest until the rent that he'd paid for this place ran out and then he'd decide what to do.

Spurius smirked. Despite his circumstances, revenge made him feel good. He slept well that night.

Three long years ago, years that felt more like ten, he'd left home to escape the poverty and drudgery that he knew would never end. The home where he was born was a small one in the poorest area of the town. It stood in a narrow alleyway well away from the rich patricians with their villas facing or near the sea, and the wealthy merchants and middle class with their fancy houses closer to the centre of town.

The upper level of the house was rented out in order to bring additional money into his family. Spurius had deliberately avoided any further contact with his father, an artisan, mother or younger sister. He resented the circumstances in which he'd been born into a decent but poor family.

Surely, he calculated, he could do better than this on his own. He left one moonless night without so much as a farewell. On the rare times when he'd seen one of his family, he'd avoided contact.

On a few occasions Spurius had come close to being caught for minor pilfering and other petty crimes. So far, he'd been fortunate not to have been apprehended, but no doubt he'd certainly been suspected. He pushed to the back of his mind the realisation that it was only a matter of time until he was caught.

Early in the morning two days later, Spurius was dragged from his bed by a couple of burly men in the service of the town's senior magistrate. He'd been identified when the dealer to whom he'd sold the pearls remembered him when questioned. He said that he'd thought the man looked shifty at the time, but didn't have any other reason to hold him or forbid the sale.

'Get your backside up!' one of the officers yelled at Spurius. 'You're on your way for a talk with the magistrate.'

'But I haven't done anything!' he whined in a futile attempt to talk his way out of trouble.

'Tell your tale to the magistrate. We don't want to hear it!'

He got a good cuff on the ear for his trouble.

Spurius was dragged up the street to the curious stares of bystanders and taken through a small, side entry to the Basilica where he was pushed onto a stone bench to await the magistrate's pleasure.

Finally, he was led into a large rectangular room with many columns where he stood facing Aquilius Publicus. He began to shake. The senior magistrate's face was stern.

'Where did you get the pearls?' Aquilius asked.

'I found them,' Spurius lied.

'And where would you have *found* them?'

'I don't remember. Maybe they'd just been dropped in the street by accident,' he added hopefully, 'or perhaps they fell off a cart?'

There was a brief laugh of incredulity from the waiting officers of the court. Aquilius frowned in annoyance.

The questioning went on for some time. The verdict of the magistrate when he returned after a very short period of deliberation, was that the prisoner was guilty of the crime of theft and deliberate destruction of property.

'You are to be imprisoned at the pleasure of this court. Take him away!' he ordered the officers holding him.

Spurius was to be incarcerated at the College of the Augustales (Curia) in the town centre. Inwardly, he cursed himself for not leaving it longer before selling the pearls.

That had been plain stupidity.

Anticipating a guilty verdict even before the questioning, magistrate Aquilius Publicus had already arranged a cell for the prisoner. It gave him considerable pleasure to have solved the case. He had no doubt that it would ease the suffering of Cassia. As for Spurius, he'd be held for a considerable period of time before being allowed his freedom again.

Herculaneum was basically a law-abiding community. There were of course, cases of petty crime, dealt with by the levy of a fine of some sort or flogging. This crime, however, involved actual destruction of property and was therefore, a level up from those. It needed to be given a more serious punishment.

The Augustales (Curia)
Decumanis Maximus

The Augustales, dedicated to the Emperor Augustus, was a building of dignity and beauty built in the central area of the town to honour him but was also used as a Curia, or Senate House. Particularly impressive was the shrine to the deified emperors inside. It held a list of the cult members. It is probable that many of them would have been freedmen.

Belonging, was considered a high honour, and included such dignitaries as Lucius Mammius Maximus and Proconsul Marcus Nonius Balbus. The inside of the hall's huge space was lightened by the presence of a large opening in the roof.

Outside, was a pedestrian-only space, with the street and those around it blocked off to carts and carriages. This, was the most important area of Herculanium.

Spurius had never been inside the Augustales before. It looked to him like the sort of place where he wouldn't feel comfortable. What he saw when he did enter, was a huge hall with an impressive central shrine. It was presently empty of occupants except for an artisan working on one of the mosaics. The walls were covered with stunning frescoes of crimson, cinnabar and blue.

He didn't have much time to stare before he was shoved roughly into a small room near the entry door. Inside, there was a bed and a wooden table. High on one wall was the only window, and this allowed a limited amount of light to filter through, but it was barred.

Spurius heard the key to the door turn in the outside lock as he was left alone inside the room. The thought ran through his mind that as long as they fed him, it was actually much better than most of the hovels he usually lived in. And at least he didn't have to sleep on the floor. Maybe things would work out after all.

Nonchalantly, he settled down on the bed to wait.

III

Later that day Aquilius Publicus walked from his office to Cassia's hotel. On the way he took the time to speak with citizens of the town who had something to discuss with him or simply to pass the time of day.

When he reached the hotel, he was told that Cassia was in her study working on the accounts. He introduced himself to the reception assistant and was asked to take a seat while she was informed. Within moments she joined him.

'Thank you for coming,' she smiled. 'Do you have news for me?'

Aquilius held out his hand revealing the pearls that had been stolen. 'I'm very pleased to be able to return these to you. I'm sorry you had to go through what you endured.'

'That's absolutely wonderful,' Cassia beamed with delight. 'Please be seated. Would you like a drink?' she offered as she gestured to a comfortable couch.

'No thank you, Cassia.'

She looked down at the pearls he'd given her and her face lit up again. 'Thank you. Who took them and destroyed my mosaic and fresco?'

They sat and talked as Aquilius recounted the evidence that had been gathered against her prior employee, Spurius, and explained where he was imprisoned. A decision on the amount of time to be served would come later.

'I'm surprised,' Cassia's expression was one of disbelief. 'He said nothing when he was dismissed, just slunk out the door and I've never seen him since.'

'That proves the point, I believe, that one never really knows what someone else is thinking.'

Cassia agreed.

At the end of their conversation, the magistrate left behind a delighted woman who unfortunately still had to pay the two fees for the repair work, but had her pearls back and could finally relax again without fear of being attacked.

Aquilius knew from experience that Cassia wouldn't forget what he'd done. When the next elections came along, that was one vote he could surely count on. He whistled an old tune he'd known for years as he strolled back to his office.

14

The Theatre

Sabina peered at her image in the mirror and frowned. She saw a round face with serious green eyes, light brown hair and a pert nose. What she didn't see was how the whole picture was transformed when she laughed or smiled. With perfect white teeth and dimples, she was unaware how pretty she looked when she was happy.

Sabina was young. She was also the daughter of Herculaneum's senior magistrate, Aquilius Publicus. Intelligent and dutiful with a serious outlook on life, it was perhaps, surprising, that her favourite leisure pursuit was attending the theatre.

On this evening she wore a long green robe, pearl earrings and a silver clip in her hair. The cosmetics on her face were subtle, as they should be, her youth needing very little adornment.

There seemed to be a particular buzz in the air and more citizens humming, singing or whistling as they walked the streets and conducted their business on this particular day. Fair skies co-operated and all seemed right with the world as the time of the afternoon performance grew nearer.

Sabina took considerable care with her appearance. As usual, she was attending with Calpurnius Piso who was Herculaneum's major theatre patron. As such, he was formerly allocated reserved seating in the most important section of the theatre close to the stage, and able to bring a guest of his choice with him if he wished.

How their understanding of attending the theatre together had begun, neither of them would have quite remembered, but it had become a natural, automatic expectation. It was not a romantic tryst, but rather a firm and very natural friendship that had begun several years before. Her father, Aquilius, preferred other pursuits and could be expected to fall asleep at most performances he went to. If required to undertake the duty of attendance, he sighed deeply and accepted that it was his burden to carry.

As for Calpurnius, he enjoyed the theatre. He looked upon Sabina as a most pleasant companion, being relaxed that he'd made his intentions quite obvious as to their type of relationship when their attendances first began. All in all, the theatre brought great joy to the town of Herculaneum. Performances took place in the afternoons.

Herculaneum's theatre was large enough to hold an audience from an average-sized town. Expensive marble statues depicting patrons were located in various parts of the theatre in which the appointments were splendid. The inside of the theatre itself was conventional in shape and freestanding, with seven exits to allow quick clearance of the crowd. Especially, if there was no orchestra, actors on stage were quite close to their audience.

Backstage, were small change rooms. Wigs, costumes of varied colours and other items such as cloaks, tunics and more were strewn haphazardly across floors and chairs, and wherever space could be found.

Make up, an important part of character portrayal was liberally used, from kohl to lamp soot and vegetable dyes. It covered every available inch of space on table tops. The whole scene was one of frantic, colourful confusion which eventually, somehow, became an enjoyable play.

Rigid social formality had recently given way to the more enjoyable sight on stage of actors without masks, a few females and singing and dancing. On this afternoon, Calpurnius and Sabina were to watch a comic Greek play by Plautus called *Miles Gloriosus* about a bragging soldier. His plays were always extremely popular and well attended.

Actors were still considered to be towards the bottom of the social ladder, not much better than the gladiators who fought in the arena. There was a huge gulf between themselves and most of those being entertained.

Light-hearted chattering and laughter filled the theatre as patrons and others attending settled in their seats. One of the actors risked a sneak peek at the audience from the wings, backstage, to ensure that everyone was ready. He rang a small bell sitting on the props table, then the curtain was removed and the entertainment began. There was hearty applause as the first character swaggered onto the stage.

In the square portico behind the stage, wine was served during intermission to patrons and their guests. For the remainder of the audience attendants offered nuts. This was one part of the evening that Sabina loved. It was an intimate opportunity to mix with the most elite of Herculaneum society and also occasionally a few of the actors. She spoke

Herculaneum: Paradise Lost

rarely but her behaviour was always impeccable and she was undoubtedly intelligent.

Those attending who laughed and left their cares behind them on that sunny afternoon, would have been shocked if they'd known that the gruesome spectre of death was already looking over their shoulders.

During the play, Calpurnius glanced across thoughtfully at Sabina. He could see that she'd obviously taken great care to present herself to best advantage in order to attend that day. Somehow the years had passed without his awareness that she was now not a girl, but an attractive young woman.

As she'd never been to his villa before, he decided that it would not be out of place for him to invite her for an after-theatre visit. He had no ulterior motive other than to see if she would be over-awed, or would feel comfortable there.

'Sabina, we must attract your father's attention before he leaves. Would you like to visit my villa just for a short time before I take you home?'

'That would be wonderful, I'd like that.' Her face lit up with pleasure.

They quickened their steps.

'Did you enjoy yourselves?' Aquilius smiled as they reached him.

'What a wonderful play,' Sabina answered, 'I laughed the whole way through it!'

'Will you give your permission, Aquilius, for me to show Sabina part of my villa this evening?' Calpurnius asked. 'I'll be sure to bring her home safely.'

'Of course. It's a good way to finish the evening,' Aquilius smiled. He turned to Sabina, 'I'll wait up for you.' He turned to look back at them as they walked away.

Calpurnius was a decent, very wealthy and highly respected man not only in Herculaneum but also in Rome. He would be considered a most suitable husband for a socially elite woman.

Despite her father's respected position in Herculaneum, Sabina and her father were not quite *that* elite.

Aquilius hardly dared to hope, as he walked away, that one day such a man would fall in love with his daughter. Time would tell.

Calpurnius and Sabina made their way through the crowd and headed up to the villa on the clifftop, the sound of the sea ever-present. Their walk was pleasant and unhurried. She was surprised when he took her elbow and steered her not into the main part of the villa, but into a smaller building to the front of the villa, also with a view of the sea.

'Here is the sea pavilion, Sabina. I thought I'd show you this tonight.'

They entered into an impressive entertaining hall. Also part of the complex, were bedrooms and a reception space. Sabina gazed at the mosaic flooring and red and white painted walls, then her glance was attracted to the Dionysian marble reliefs inserted into wall niches. She slowly approached them, fascinated.

For a few moments Calpurnius stood back, saying nothing, pleased by her obvious interest in the reliefs. Coming to her side he explained their meaning and answered the questions that she asked.

'They're really beautiful!' she said, softly.

In the lamplight, her eyes shining as she smiled up at him, Calpurnius felt an attraction that was a rare experience for him. Moving away a little from her, he pointed out several other features of the pavilion, then they sat talking.

'It's late, Sabina, I'd better take you home to your father,' he stated after a short time.

'Thank you, Calpurnius, I've enjoyed our time together immensely,' she answered.

They returned to the town and Calpurnius knocked for entry as they reached the door of Aquilius' house, a couple of streets behind the sea. He was thoughtful as he made his way back to the villa. His need for an heir had become much stronger in recent years. He considered Sabina's suitability as a possible partner, but she was not of his social standing.

Nonetheless, he found himself attracted to her, and after all, he lived not in Rome with its rigid class society, but the sleepy town of Herculaneum. There was no doubt that she was a virtuous and intelligent woman, which was more than could be said for many of the high-born women of Rome with their promiscuous ways and greedy ambition. They were exactly the types of women who would attempt to lure him into marriage, attracted mainly by his wealth.

It just might be that he and Sabina would be a good match. Yes, it was certainly possible.

One thing Calpurnius did know, however, was that once he started down that path he could never turn back. He hadn't missed her look of admiration when she'd gazed up at him. He decided that he'd take his time and very, very slowly, step by step, consider progressing the relationship to another level. He'd make sure that he never hurt her.

Part III

Storm Clouds Gather

15

HERCULANEUM

The Augustales

Storm clouds, thick and heavy, grew blacker by the minute as they rolled in. Racing across the sky they rapidly approached the town. At first, just a few huge drops of rain fell, then lightening ripped the clouds apart as claps of thunder shook the sky in fury. Residents walking in the streets ran for cover as a torrent of pelting rain slapped onto the hard, volcanic street paving stones. They sheltered in any public buildings or private porticoes they could find.

Spurius sat up abruptly as the door to his room was opened and the usual attendant thumped a plate of food down on the table as well as a beaker. He moved to the plate, picked up the food and inspected it closely. As he'd thought, it was once more, one of only a few choices they kept serving to him over and over again.

A few pieces of sorry-looking fruit lay on an old plate along with one tiny, plain pastry as well as a very small piece of stale fish. The whole lot looked particularly unappetising.

'Any chance of diluting the wine less tonight?' Spurius grumbled as he looked down at the beaker. 'This stuff might as well all be water!' The boredom of his existence was beginning to irritate him. He'd buried memories of his former existence when he'd had very little food or wine and sometimes, none at all.

'You'll receive an official notification regarding your situation later tomorrow,' the attendant informed him sourly. 'Rumour has it that your sentence has just been reviewed. The senior magistrate has decided to add an additional three months to your sentence because of your attitude. There will be no unwatered wine tonight, so appreciate what you have. Get used to it!'

Glancing through the partially open door, Spurius could see a group of well attired men who appeared to be having some sort of a meeting. Spurious got no more than a brief glimpse of them.

The attendant decided to leave. He was becoming irritated by the prisoner's constant whinging. It wasn't as if he had a perfect life himself. 'At least you're dry in here,' he growled. 'It's a real deluge outside. I feel sorry tonight for those who don't even have a room.'

Spurius waved his hand in a rude gesture of dismissal and didn't bother to reply. The door to his room was shut once more and locked. Earlier in his imprisonment, he'd already pulled the table across to the window and climbed on top of it, in order to inspect the bars on it. He found to his anger that they were strong and secure. There was no way that he could move them. He was going nowhere!

Three more months.

Herculaneum: Paradise Lost

It was outrageous!

III

The Piso Villa

Calpurnius had invited Sabina to his villa for dinner. A table had been especially set with silver cups, bowls and candelabra and it was laden with the first course of fine food, to be replaced with many others as required. The perfume of roses hung in the air and the lamps were lit. Sabina arrived just prior to the beginning of the storm.

They would dine alone, unchaperoned.

Sabina looked gorgeous. Little did Calpurnius realise how much time had been taken and how much money spent by Aquilius on selecting the extraordinary gown she wore as well as on her hair, perfume and cosmetics.

Taking inspiration from the Greek decoration in the seaside pavilion, father and daughter had decided on a long, pure white chiton of soft silken material. It was slim and fitting. Around her waist she wore a gold woven belt. The robe was caught with a golden clip at one shoulder. Her earrings were of gold and her hair encased in a net woven with gold and silver threads. On her feet she wore elaborate sandals.

Leia welcomed her at the door with grace and a smile, bowing slightly. Little did the woman before her realise how much the slave would have given to stand in her place. Leia escorted her to the reception room and Calpurnius rose to receive his guest.

What he saw pleased him greatly. He smiled broadly at her. 'Sabina, I'm so pleased you accepted my invitation. You look exquisite.'

'Thank you, Calpurnius. It is my pleasure to be here.'

Servants drew back their chairs to seat them and the meal began. As time passed, their conversation progressed from being slightly formal to far more casual, interspersed with laughter. Sabina had been well educated and conversed without difficulty on the subjects raised.

It had taken Calpurnius many nights of troubled decision-making to progress down the path he'd finally chosen. This was a very good beginning, he thought, as the meal finished and they sat together on a couch with refreshing cups of frozen ice flavoured with lemon. There was a feeling of being almost in a dream, in a semi-lit and intimate area set aside towards the windows looking out across the sea. The storm had passed.

Before long, Calpurnius took Sabina's hand. 'Would you like to see the rest of the villa?' he offered.

'Yes. I'd really enjoy that.'

They went from room to room and Sabina's eyes widened in wonder. She'd never seen such wealth and extravagance before. They walked out towards the gardens, appreciating the scene before them, lit here and there with lamps.

'What an extraordinary estate you have,' Sabina said in awe. 'Everywhere there is nothing that is not perfection.'

Calpurnius turned Sabina to face him then bent and gently kissed her. She responded to him and his second kiss was longer and more passionate.

They drew apart and placing his arm around her waist, Calpurnius guided her back towards the front of the villa. He felt the same desire for her as he'd experienced at the seaside pavilion. Perhaps, he'd found the girl with whom he'd spend the remainder of his life. She seemed capable of enjoying the things that were important in him.

Aquilius was overjoyed to hear what had happened from Sabina when she returned to him that night. He believed that Calpurnius was not a man to trifle with a young woman's affections. Now, father and daughter could only wait and hope that future events would draw Calpurnius and Sabina even closer together.

As she lay in her bed that night, Sabina's heart was racing.

She barely dared hope that anything would come from her interlude that night with Calpurnius. She was strongly attracted to him and it seemed that the feeling was mutual. Still, she reasoned, he would surely marry someone from a higher social class than herself.

Careful and a little hesitant by nature, Sabina could see no reason why Calpurnius would have teased her that way, however, if all that tonight had been about was friendship. But, how would she ever cope with being mistress of such a vast estate, even if he did propose to her? The last thing she'd ever want to do would be to embarrass him and for that matter, herself, by letting him down.

16

The Hotel (Albergo)
Cardo 111

Cassia smiled to herself as she saw Prima step down from her carriage. True to her word, she'd arrived once more to stay again at the hotel.

'It's good to have you here Prima,' Cassia greeted her. 'If you're not too tired, once you're settled, meet me in the reception area and we can enjoy some small snacks together.'

'It was quite dusty on the way here today, so I'm really ready to freshen up in my room,' Prima answered. 'I'll be with you in just a few minutes.'

Prima had been given the same room as on her prior visit, which pleased her. It was easier when travelling if everything felt familiar. Having splashed cool water on her face and dried it as well as washing her hands, she re-joined Cassia and sank gratefully down into the couch beside her.

'I suppose it's been quiet here?' Prima enquired casually.

'Yes. Although we did have a terrible storm one night.'

'No strangers around much to worry anyone about with robberies and crime?' Prima quizzed Cassia.

'Funny you should ask about that.'

Prima raised a questioning eyebrow.

'Well, there was one stranger I saw going into the inn near old Numerius' silversmith shop. 'I don't think I've ever seen that man in town before,' Cassia replied. 'I wouldn't have even noticed, except that I've been more watchful since the incident that happened to me recently while you were last here.'

'Yes, that was absolutely terrible,' Prima commiserated with her. 'Anyway, at least everything is looking perfect again thanks to Frontius. I'm sure it was probably only a visiting worker on holiday that you saw that day outside the inn.'

'Yes, although I can't explain why that worried me,' Cassia continued thoughtfully, 'except that it was a bit strange, he seemed quite flustered and eager to disappear inside. Initially, I'd particularly noticed him because he had very fair hair.'

Prima nodded then changed the subject. They sat chatting for a while longer during which time she ascertained that the town had been quiet since her last visit. Nothing of any note appeared to have happened. Finishing the small delicacies on her plate, she returned to her room to change for dinner.

The next morning, after breakfast, Prima prepared to leave the hotel.

'I'm going to do some shopping,' she mentioned to Cassia as she left, 'then I'd like to walk on the beach.'

'Enjoy yourself!' Cassia called out and waved.

A short walk brought Prima to the sand. She'd never ventured there on her prior visits.

She stepped onto the black, volcanic beach not far from the suburban bathhouse and the sand scrunched between her toes. She noticed the open vaulted structures that fronted onto it and counted twelve or so of them. Inside, they were presently empty, and she guessed that they were boathouses. The fishermen were just finishing their work for the day. The largest boats could be pulled up onto a man-made slipway.

Pausing, Prima walked up the six steps leading from the sand to the Shrine of Venus which stood beside the boat sheds, and studied the luxurious white marble with a black and white mosaic floor that met her gaze. She liked its location right beside the sea. It seemed appropriate, somehow, to have a small, intimate temple here, secluded yet inviting. Perhaps the fishermen drew comfort knowing as they put out to sea, that the goddess watched over their safety.

Prima looked up briefly at Vesuvius, a huge hulking mass looming over them, noticing the vineyards and their green lushness. She'd tasted the local *Vesuviano* wine and it was very good indeed.

The ocean looked appealing but she reminded herself sternly that now was not the time to relax and dream by the water.

She had a job to do.

Prima continued to walk until she was looking at the entry to the vast estate that loomed above her on the clifftop. Another day, she decided, she'd find out more about it.

She walked back into the town. Having asked for directions from the owner of one of the shops on her way, she deliberately walked past the silversmith's shop, then sauntered more slowly by the inn a few doors away, quickly glancing inside the open door. The small reception room was empty.

On the opposite side of the street was a trinket shop. Prima wandered over and spent a long time looking at the jewellery on offer. It was of an inexpensive type none of which was personally appealing to her.

She was just about to leave when she noticed a dishevelled-looking man step quickly into the inn. He looked like the same type of man that Cassia had described, except that he had dark hair.

She frowned. The situation was becoming interesting.

The Temple of Isis
(Unexcavated)

While Prima was out "shopping" Cassia kept the vow she'd made to herself to visit the Temple of Isis. She'd been there before, but she always seemed these days to have little time to spare to visit it as often as she would have liked.

Leaving the hotel, she walked the short distance to the temple, enjoying the fresh air. It was in a quiet location, further from the foreshore and vendors' shops. As she approached, she saw that a ceremony had just finished.

It was rumoured that the water used in all of the temple's ceremonies was actually transported from Egypt and stored in a tunnel under the site.

The high priest was turning to re-enter the temple interior and she noticed the remains of a fire lit in a large, ceremonial bowl. It stood on top of a low, marble pillar in the courtyard, where the fire was still smouldering. Priests, with their heads shaven, wearing long, white robes talked together quietly in a group as the priestesses, most of them young also gathered together. One of the young women saw Cassia approaching and went to greet her.

'Cassia, we haven't seen you for a while,' she welcomed her.

'The hotel has been very busy,' Cassia explained, 'and there's been some trouble for the magistrate to clear up for us.'

The girl hesitated. 'Is everything normal again now?'

'Fortunately, it is,' Cassia reassured her. 'I've come to give thanks to the goddess.'

'Please, come into the temple then I'll leave you to pray to Isis in peace.'

The priestess took Cassia's hand, and together they mounted the many steps leading up to the impressive front porch. She gestured to Cassia to enter then left her as promised.

Although Cassia had been inside before, it never ceased to awake in her a feeling of awe. Quiet, and filled with corners of shadow and light, it was like entering another world.

There was a strong smell of incense.

She sat silently gazing around the temple's interior.

The deities of Egypt gazed back at Cassia as she surveyed the wall paintings. She looked first to Isis and bowed her head before her. Then she sat and marvelled at her favourite, Hathor, goddess of music, as well as Anubis, the fearful god of death who stared coldly back at her.

Frescoes of the figures of Sobek the crocodile god, Maat and other gods and goddesses had been painted there, as well as delightful, delicate pink flamingos. Nile river scenes featured vividly on the colourful walls, depicting scenes of Egyptians using shadoofs to draw water from the river for irrigation.

The temple held within it the heady fragrance of lotus blossoms. It had the effect of intoxicating the senses and removing the harshness of reality. Time ceased to matter and a sensation of peace prevailed.

There was no one else inside. The high priest had already departed.

Cassia sat appreciating the stillness. How long she was there she didn't know by the time she finally emerged back out into the sunshine. But she did appreciate that she really felt calm after praying in this place.

As another glorious day ended in Herculaneum, Cassia was aware, walking back to the hotel, that she was in a place in her inner self where she felt more genuinely happy than she'd ever done before in her life.

It was something for which to be truly grateful.

17

The Bakery (Pistrinum)
Cardo V

A shabby beggar slouched against the front wall outside the bakery shop owned by Sextus Patulcus Felix, next door to the wine shop. He'd had his fair share or more of luck in life, enough to gain him the affectionate name of "lucky." He was famous for his cakes.

It was early in the day and the aroma of freshly baked bread and his specialty cakes was mouth-watering and almost overwhelming in its appeal. The beggar's eyes appeared to be half-closed, perhaps from fatigue, or maybe intoxication. He smelt strongly of wine and held out his grimy hand hoping for coins with which to buy breakfast. So far, no one had taken pity on the unkempt beggar.

Prima saw him and crossed the road to speak to him.

'You'd be better off living at an inn,' she suggested softly.

'Can you recommend the right one?' he mumbled. 'I'm going to need a room but also a drink soon. The public water fountains are crowded with people standing around talking and they don't seem to like me being there.'

'Certainly,' she added. 'I know of a couple of men who live at the inn near the silversmith's shop.'

'But I may need other help,' the beggar confided in her quietly, 'otherwise I mightn't be strong enough to manage.' His intelligent eyes looked directly into hers.

'I'll arrange some for you,' Prima replied as she bent to place a coin in his hand. She walked on without looking back and disappeared around the corner. Finding a messenger, she wrote a short, urgent note to the commander of the Praetorian Guard at the fort at Nuceria, and dispatched it immediately.

Prima had done her job. Secretly on the Emperor's payroll, she seemed an unlikely spy, but she'd proved highly effective in the past. Some minutes later, she walked back towards Cletus, who was still sitting outside the bakery. Prima walked by without even looking at him. As she passed by she whispered, 'all is well.'

She continued up the street, pausing only to glance at the fruit displayed outside the shop of Aulus Fuferus, then she walked on, humming happily as she did so. The shopkeeper noticed her. He stood outside his shop watching the beautiful woman saunter by until she disappeared from sight.

Not long after that the beggar left.

Nearby, at the inn near the silversmith's shop, Atticus breathed a sigh of relief as Quintus tapped on the door of his room then entered. He threw his bag onto the bed and sank down into the nearest couch looking as if he hadn't slept for a very long time.

'Thank the gods that's over!' he exclaimed.

'I'm glad you got my message,' Atticus told him, 'what happened to you?'

'I've never been so scared in my life! The guards caught me on the island and took me to Rome. I have to admit I was speechless with fear. Finally, they dragged me in front of Titus. I was left sweating for some time before he turned up. The only good thing about it all is that at least he let me go.'

'Titus interrogated you?'

'Yes. I couldn't believe it. Once I saw him and realised who it was, I thought I'd end up being one of those men who disappears never to be seen again. There must be a lot of gold for it to be that important.'

'But, why did he let you go?' Atticus asked, his voice tinged with suspicion.

'He said I wasn't carrying a weapon or doing anything wrong when they caught me.'

Atticus nodded, satisfied.

'We do still have one major problem though,' Quintus said thoughtfully.

'What's that?' Atticus frowned.

'What if we need money to buy tools?'

'We do have some coins,' Atticus reminded him.

'Yes, but we'll need that to pay for our rooms here.'

The two men sat in silence, pondering an answer to their problem.

'Maybe, we should look for a few hours of work,' Quintus suggested.

'That would solve our problem, but we don't know the town.'

'We'll ask at the reception desk. They should be able to tell us where to try.

The next night, having been given directions from the owner of the inn, Quintus and Atticus walked through the streets at dusk until they came to a slovenly looking bar in a questionable part of town. It fronted straight onto a mean alleyway.

There were only a couple of old men inside drinking when they arrived and walked directly up to the counter.

'We'd like to talk to Rufus,' Quintus stated.

'Who's asking?'

'My name's Quintus and my friend here is Atticus.'

'Wait here. I'll see if he's available.'

A few minutes later, a large man of middle age came through from the back and approached them with a scowl. 'What do you want?'

'Just a few hours of work,' Quintus replied.

For a few moments the owner, Rufus, stood looking them up and down before he spoke.

'Can you keep your mouths shut?' he grunted.

'Of course,' Atticus assured him.

'Then you're in luck. There's a small job I need done and by the look of you both, you're strong enough to manage it. Follow me.'

He led the way through the filthy partition and into the back of the bar. Entering, he pointed to something large bulging under a cheap, old coverlet.

'This man is dead.' Rufus stated the obvious as he removed the covering and they saw a body.

Quintus and Atticus stood speechless.

'Well, do you want the job or not?'

'What do we need to do?' Atticus squeaked, eventually finding his voice.

'I'll give you a handcart. Take it to the necropolis. It's dark enough now, dig a grave and bury him. Afterwards, come back and I'll pay you well for your trouble.'

Quintus and Atticus looked at each other.

'We need the money. We'll do it,' Quintus shrugged.

18

Cletus arrived at the Piso villa having reverted to his normal appearance. His knock brought Leia then Calpurnius to the door. The agent handed over his identification.

'Calpurnius, my name is Cletus. I'm one of Titus' undercover men and I'll be working jointly with the commander of the fort at Nuceria. I believe you're in need of assistance. Titus has handled the details of this mission. Hopefully, we'll put the scum planning to rob Rome of her gold out of action and where they belong.'

'Come in, Cletus. I've been wondering since receiving Titus' note just what could be done. It's a great relief to see you. What does he have planned?'

Having seated themselves comfortably, Cletus brought Calpurnius up to date on the latest events that had occurred. This left him suitably surprised.

'I expect that these two rogues will attempt to gain entry to your villa,' Cletus continued. 'After all, there's really nowhere else in town that the gold could be kept except here. It may sound surprising, but I think we should help them. There is an element of risk, but I believe we can cope with that.'

Calpurnius raised an eyebrow but remained silent, allowing the more experienced of the two of them to take the lead.

'The last thing we want is for anyone to be injured. If they're cornered there are no guarantees that these men won't become violent. I propose that you have your caretaker remove himself from his cottage at sunset and come here, after unlocking but closing the gates to the back garden of the villa. I'm hoping that if they decide to enter that way, they'll think he's gone for a break and forgotten to lock the gate.

Now, let's have a look at the locks on the outside door leading into the room with the gold. I'll also need to walk around the gardens so I know where everything is and how much ground there is to cover. Then, I can advise the commander of the fort at Nuceria how many men to send. He's already been alerted to the situation.'

Cletus nodded in approval as he inspected the variety of locks that Calpurnius had already placed on the door for protection. It would take some time for thieves to remove them.

'There's no way they can get in here without the proper equipment and making considerable noise as well. At the moment they don't know anything, so no doubt they'll just come the first time thinking they'll have a look around without any problem, then sneak out again.

The gold shipment that left the Sacred Island to come here on the night that Quintus was caught, is due to arrive in Herculaneum either tonight or tomorrow night. They've almost certainly worked that out as they knew what the destination was.'

For a few moments Cletus stood absolutely still, gazing out over the sea. Then, he smiled.

Herculaneum: Paradise Lost

'This is what we're going to do…'

Once again, a Roman boat slipped quietly into the inlet outside the villa. As expected, all was quiet and still. The trees threw dark shadows, silent and sombre across the grass, as Marcus and his men clambered out into the water and moments later, reached the shore.

As usual, Silvanus held a flare aloft to light their way.

'This is the last of it, at least for the moment,' Marcus informed Calpurnius.

'Well, let's get to it and carry it into the storeroom.'

The legionaries struggled to drag the chests to the door. There were fewer chests this time, for safety, if nothing else, in case if the worst happened, there would be less to steal. The gold was soon stowed away with the rest.

There was an absolute fortune hidden in the small room.

Marcus' voice was almost a whisper. 'No problems yet?' He glanced across at Calpurnius.

'No. But I believe it's only a matter of time. The men have been seen in town.'

'Are you sure you don't want my legionaries to stay?' Marcus asked hesitantly, 'it sounds as if there's going to be plenty of trouble. Who knows how much?'

'No, my friend, but thanks for the offer. I believe we have everything in hand. The best thing we can do right now is to keep things looking as normal as possible.'

'May fortune be with you,' Marcus murmured.

Soon, he and his legionaries had departed.

An oversized moon clung to the sky as shadows flittered, unseen, through the streets of Herculaneum. No lamp lights could be seen and citizens of the town slept. Dark figures, one by one, moved quickly along laneways past shopfronts, bars, and houses, staying close to buildings, some spilling out onto the sandy beachfront. Not as much as a word gave warning of their presence.

The gates to the Piso villa opened with a slight creak. Closing the gates behind them, the guards spread out taking up their assigned places, melding back into the trees and the walls of the villa, but staying clear of the room with the gold. Others guarded the seafront entry near the pool.

They waited.

A short time later, having decided to check out the villa grounds and see if they could find any hints as to where the gold was stored, Quintus and Atticus entered by way of the beach, having agreed that going in through the front gate would be too dangerous. They saw and heard no one. Atticus carried a small, hand held lamp which gave a tiny light.

First, they quickly circled the villa which stood in darkness. Then, they began to search in more detail. It wasn't long before they found the door situated on the ground floor not far from the pool.

'Look,' Quintus whispered to Atticus in excitement as he caught sight of the locks. 'Hold the lamp closer. No one has this many locks on a ground floor garden room for nothing. There's something important in there.'

'But how will we ever get the locks off?'

'We'll have to come back tomorrow night with tools. If we're careful we won't be heard,' Quintus continued softly. 'At least, I hope we can get them off easily.'

They peered at the door through the darkness, holding the locks in their hands in an attempt to assess how sturdy they were.

'Don't move or you're dead!' The stern command rang clearly through the stillness.

Quintus and Atticus found themselves surrounded by praetorian guards. They shrank back against the villa walls. The thought went through Quintus' mind that this time, he certainly had been caught in a criminal act and had no chance of talking his way out of it. They were escorted by the light of flares carried by guards, through the town and out through the walls.

Caged in a barred cart allowing no chance of escape, the two men were bumped around on rough roads all the way to the fort at Nuceria. Once there, no one heard a word from them ever again.

Life in Herculaneum returned to normal.

Soon after the Emperor, Vespasian, died. He was succeeded by his son, Titus.

19

One month later

The small town of Herculaneum lay dozing peacefully in the sun, its gardens perfumed by sweet but deadly pink oleander blossoms, its people going about their business and enjoying simple pleasures by the sea. Fishermen coaxed the many fresh seafood treasures from the water, satisfied with their generous catch.

The gold hidden in the Piso villa had recently been removed by Titus as the final stages of building and decoration were drawing near at the huge Flavian amphitheatre. Calpurnius breathed a sigh of relief at being relieved of any responsibility for it.

Frontius was close to finishing the latest fresco he was painting for one of the villa's walls and his model, Helena, had become betrothed to one of the town's young men. She was so besotted with him that he filled her every waking moment with thoughts of love, and she no longer gossiped about most of the other people in the town or events going on around her.

Livia grew more sour by the minute but her husband, Vennidius, rarely noticed her, or the black walls that he hated in his house and they remained as Frontius had left them.

It appeared to those few who knew him well, that Vennidius had recently become close to another woman, (also already married), who was attractive, even if a little larger than ideal and who laughed a great deal.

Her name was Florina. They kept their relationship very private. For once, Vennidius was glad that Livia had so little contact with others in the town. Of course, it also helped that Florina was Livia's only real friend and *she* wasn't saying anything.

Spurius still languished in the small locked room at the Augustales, but was coming towards the end of his imprisonment. He yelled and shouted more whenever anyone came near him, and on this morning had eaten only part of his breakfast.

It seemed to magistrate Aquilius Publicus, that he had less cases of crime to contend with, which left him more welcome time to relax at home.

Cassia continued to manage her hotel with pleasure, especially when it was time for Prima to return, and the two women became firm friends. The summer had been hot but there was a cooler feeling in the air that announced that the season of autumn was approaching.

Calpurnius had made an appointment to visit Aquilius at his home. The day was drawing to a close as he rang for entry at the front door. Aquilius opened it himself when he heard the bell tinkle.

'Come in, Calpurnius,' he smiled. 'It's good to see you again. I trust that you're well?'

'I am. And you?'

'Older than I could wish, but one cannot question the will of the gods.'

Aquilius ushered Calpurnius into the large reception room and gestured to him to sit. 'Will you have a cup of wine with me?'

'Certainly. It's kind of you.'

There was no sign of Sabina.

'Perhaps you have guessed at the reason for my visit today?' Calpurnius began.

'Perhaps,' Aquilius replied smiling slightly, 'but I will let you raise the matter your own way and in your own time.'

'I know that Sabina's young, but I love your daughter, and it seems that I'm fortunate that her feelings for me are returned. Aquilius, I've come to ask if you will allow a betrothal between us. I realise there are questions you may wish to ask. If so, please do.'

'I have no questions, Calpurnius. I've known of your reputation for many years, and most of all I've seen the two of you together. It's obvious that your friendship over the years has blossomed into love. I consider it an honour that you have chosen my daughter. She's a girl with a loving heart and I know that you'll treat her well. You have my permission and I wish you both every happiness. I will leave it to you to tell her.'

Aquilius stood and held out his hand to Calpurnius. An agreement had been reached. As he made his way back to his villa, Calpurnius was surprised at the relief he felt. Perhaps unaware of it, he'd actually been a little nervous. He certainly had no doubt, however, that Sabina was the woman he wanted to be with forever.

To celebrate the announcement of the betrothal, Calpurnius invited anyone who was a resident of Herculaneum to attend a celebration party on the grounds of his estate. The goodwill shown towards him and also to Sabina was evident.

There was a hum of excitement throughout the town and everyone turned to the question of outfitting themselves in the best clothes they owned or could afford to buy. The clothmaker's business accelerated considerably. Most of the women wore the latest fashion of pastel colours and once they'd all gathered in the back garden of the villa, it looked like what it was – a contented and rather excited group of people in all the colours of the rainbow.

Long tables were laden with a huge variety of food with enough to feed an army. Slaves served the guests, continually refilling their cups with wine.

Towards the end of the afternoon, Calpurnius, holding Sabina's hand, made a speech thanking those attending for coming and wishing them all the blessings of the goddess Fortuna.

As the couple stood together in that glorious setting with a look of sheer happiness on their faces, the gods seemed to be smiling down upon them.

The applause from their guests was generous and they looked on indulgently as the couple kissed. As the sun sank over the red rim of the horizon, people began to depart and return to their homes.

The happy couple retreated inside the villa, tired but excited. Soon, they'd set the date for their wedding.

Events were soon to occur that would cause them to look back to this day as one of peace and joy, the memory of which would be sorely needed.

Lorraine Blundell

INVITATION

The Palatine Hill
The Royal Palace

4th October 79 A.D.

Titus Caesar, Emperor of Rome, requests the presence of Lucius Calpurnius Piso and Sabina Publicus at a private, official dinner. Dress will be formal. The date set for the occasion is the 16th October.

Calpurnius smiled as he read the invitation. Sabina was overwhelmed when he showed it to her. Her first thought was what on earth was she going to wear? Her father and Calpurnius laughed. It was wonderful to see her so happy.

Prima was relaxing in the reception room of the hotel when Cassia personally handed a scroll to her which had just arrived by messenger. She had turned to go when Prima called her back.

'Cassia, have a look at this!' Prima handed the scroll back to her and she had to read it twice before she could believe it. 'I'm so pleased for you. I think it's incredible!' Cassia exclaimed.

Privately, Prima was amazed and grateful that as a woman of such low social class she could be so accepted by the Emperor. She began to cry.

'I hope they're happy tears,' Cassia smiled as the two hugged.

'They're tears of pure joy!' Prima responded. 'The way of life I've chosen has rewarded me well, but I've always had a cloud hanging over me in terms of being accepted because of my low social standing.'

Cassia kissed her cheek. 'Prima, never think less of yourself than you should,' she told her. 'There are many who appear to be above both of us in social standing but who are anything but honest and decent people.'

In Rome, Cletus wondered what his commanding officer wanted when he received a summons to go to his office. He had no memory of having committed an offence of any kind. It was possible, though, that there was a job that needed special attention that he wished to discuss with him.

Still, it wasn't an everyday occurrence.

'Come in, Cletus. I've been requested to pass this on to you in person. I've been informed as to the document's content and I have to say I believe you thoroughly deserve it. Well done! You're dismissed. You may read it at your leisure.'

Cletus returned down the hallway to his room where he sat down on the bed and opened the parchment. A look of astonishment spread across his face.

This would be the memory of a lifetime.

20

ROME

The Palatine Hill
The Royal Palace

Prima was the last to arrive. She came by litter. Her reaction to the surroundings was much the same as that of all who had ever been fortunate enough to find sufficient favour to gain entry to the gardens of the royal palace. She stood gazing around her entranced by the vast lawn, subtle lights and creatively placed brilliantly coloured statues.

Not a sound intruded into the silence, except for the gushing of water and the songs of the birds.

The central fountain standing in the garden directly in front of the official palace entrance, was unlike anything she'd ever seen before. It was elaborate and cleverly illuminated. At its centre, water gushed from a cherub's mouth into the air high above, falling down again with a delightful splash.

Perfume from myriad blossoms fragranced the air. Prima breathed in deeply of the heady scents that stimulated her senses.

She looked up at the sky at a crescent moon and stars that seemed like pinpricks of silver. They seemed to cover the entirety of the night sky.

There was a slight smile on the face of the guard who came down the steps to speak to her. His voice was clipped and official but extremely courteous.

'Salve. May I ask your name.'

'My name is Prima.'

'Welcome. Please follow me.'

He led her into the first reception room. Cletus, Calpurnius and Sabina were already seated on comfortable couches talking and rose to meet her.

'I still have the coin you so generously gave me outside the bakery,' Cletus grinned, enjoying the memory.

Prima laughed. 'Did you spend it? I was only hoping that you weren't as hungry as you looked. I must admit you did a great job of disguising yourself. That's even more obvious now that I can see what you really look like.' She didn't feel it was appropriate to add that she was surprised how handsome she thought he was.

'That's one of the drawbacks of my job,' Cletus agreed. 'But, it's not good for my morale leaving people with such a bad impression of me.'

Animated discussion followed for several minutes after which they were invited to follow one of the staff dressed in royal livery to the room in which they were to dine with the Emperor.

They walked on cool marble floors that seemed to go on forever. Lamps provided intimate lighting and vibrant rugs from the east in luscious colours added warmth and vivacity.

Stationed outside the windows, guards kept careful watch with others patrolling the gardens and entries.

There was nothing ordinary about that evening.

Before they reclined for dinner, they were requested to present themselves in a line just before Titus entered. His eyes twinkled as he passed by each of them in turn.

'This is indeed a pleasant duty! Cletus, well done! Tonight, I present you with the Award of Valour for your duties in protecting what rightfully belongs to Rome. I wouldn't be at all surprised, either, if your commanding officer found himself in a position to grant you a much deserved promotion!' The Emperor pinned the medal on him and Cletus stepped back.

Titus moved on to face Calpurnius and embraced him. 'I cannot thank you enough for providing safe refuge for the gold that will complete Rome's masterpiece. It became a dangerous situation. Fortunately, what was a very real threat was handled superbly. Please accept this fresco for your personal villa.'

'Thank you, Caesar.' Calpurnius took possession of a large, rolled package. It was later found to be an original fresco painted by the famous Roman painter, Fabullus.

Sabina was introduced to the Emperor. Her eyes shone with happiness and she looked up at him shyly. He gave her a fatherly smile. 'I wish you every happiness, Sabina, you are betrothed to a man of outstanding decency and courage, but I'm sure you already know that.'

Titus moved on to the final person in the line.

'And you must be Prima!' He placed his hand on her shoulder. 'You're a woman of great beauty equalled only by your courage and skill in the tasks you have undertaken secretly for Rome, especially the latest one. You have my thanks. There is a small but charming house on the Esquiline Hill for which, tomorrow, you will be given the deeds of ownership. I hope you will continue to serve when danger threatens the Empire.'

Prima smiled up at Titus. Her pleasure was obvious. 'It

would be my honour to do so,' she answered. 'I cannot find the words to thank you enough for your generous gift.'

One final announcement remained.

'I invite you to sleep in the palace overnight. Rooms have been allocated for each of you. You're welcome to enjoy the gardens should you wish to do so. I know, Cletus, that you'd prefer to return to the familiar lodgings at your barracks, but please feel free to look around the palace as much as you wish before you go. Now, I believe it's time we enjoyed dinner before we all starve.'

Titus gestured to a small group of musicians waiting in a corner of the room and they began to play softly. An extravagant dinner was served surrounded by adornments of great beauty. Held under the spell of the music, flowers, dim lighting and the pleasure of the occasion, the guests' inhibitions dropped away. Titus was a considerate and highly likeable host. It was a time of joy to be remembered in the terrible events yet to come.

Cletus walked alone in the palace gardens before sitting on a bench to reflect on the evening and his future. He loved the challenge of the undercover work he did, but he was close to a decision whether he needed to retire and marry. He wondered what his future held.

This evening had been one that he would always remember with pride. He rose and walked down away from the Palatine and through the Forum.

His destination was the praetorian guard barracks not far from the new amphitheatre. It was special accommodation with an apartment for the commander, and fourteen other spacious and well-furnished rooms for elite members of Rome's guards.

Cletus, as the top undercover agent undertaking the most dangerous of missions, was housed there. Especially now that the Emperor and many of his advisors were of a military background, they made sure that those of their own kind were well looked after.

Intricate mosaic floors and a comfortable bed welcomed him back. He no sooner lay down then he fell into a deep sleep, his dreams taking him back to Herculaneum.

Prima, Calpurnius and Sabina lingered in the palace gardens talking, laughing softly and looking around in awe. For Calpurnius, himself the owner of a beautiful estate, the sights and sounds around him perfumed by hundreds of blossoms was still a special experience to behold and more impressive. As for Sabina, she had little to say, overcome with the sensual sensations around her and the evening's dinner.

All of them returned and were shown to their rooms by one of the guards where they each found on their pillows a bag of gold coins. Cletus had been handed his before leaving, and knew that this was one more step towards his future financial security.

Only intimacy between them was missing for Calpurnius and Sabina, not possible by accepted custom, until after their marriage. But both slumbered, knowing that their dreams would soon be realised.

Part IV

PARADISE LOST

21

HERCULANEUM

17th October 79 A.D.

Herculaneum awoke from sleep to swaying palm trees, a sun-drenched beach and the sound of shops of every kind opening for business for the day. The summer had been long, hot and parched, with mild, ongoing earth tremors but water was readily available. There were rumours, however, that Pompeii nearby was struggling to maintain its water supplies.

A quietly confident normality pervaded the town and there was a feeling of languorous happiness. Its inhabitants had long ago forgotten, which would be to their cost, that the volcano that menaced those who lived beneath it had been active and still was. As usual, greenery and vines covered the sides of the looming hulk of Vesuvius as it watched over the citizens, not that anyone particularly looked up at it on that warm morning in early autumn.

At the hotel owned by Cassia, morning breakfast was underway with servants busy as usual. The clink of quality Samian tableware filled the air as well as the carefree chatter of staff assisting those guests who were leaving. For a while there was an increase in those exiting normally through the walls that enclosed the town. Some would seek to travel to Pompeii, others to Napoli and still more back to Rome.

Decius sat contentedly at breakfast at his usual thermopolium looking out at the sea where the fishermen were just about to finish for the day, their work done, as he enjoyed his pastry and gossiping with his friend, the owner, Justus.

'I've almost decided to take the day off work,' he grinned lazily.

'No such luck for me,' Justus grumbled. 'I have to stay open just in case a customer comes in. Otherwise, I'll be getting complaints!'

Further from the beach, Felix Patulcus at the bakery, had just prepared bread and would soon place it in his oven, protected by the phallic symbol above it. He patted it fondly for good luck before doing so.

Next door, Aulus Fuferus set up a display of fruit in front of his shop and stood enjoying the sunshine. 'Let us hope we both do well today!' Aulus raised his voice expansively as he smiled across at Felix. 'Sales have actually been quite good lately I have to admit.'

He disappeared back into his shop.

'I'm going out shopping as soon as breakfast is finished,' Livia informed her husband, Vennidius, at the House of the Black Saloon adjacent to the Decumanus Maximus nearby. 'One of the servants will prepare your lunch for you if you're still here, but I may not return in time to join you.' She also still had to apply her cosmetics before she left, and that always took time so she hurried to complete the task.

Livia's friend, Florina, at the House of the Stags was still sleeping deeply, having entertained friends from Rome until very late the night before.

She would sleep into eternity.

Senior magistrate, Aquilius Publicus, had also just finished breakfast at his home. He settled himself at his desk to write the morning's correspondence, and was looking forward to Sabina's return to hear her account of the dinner with the Emperor. He gazed out of the window at what appeared to be a beautiful day. Perhaps, he decided, he might take a short walk soon for a while to enjoy it before going to the Basilica. He'd been kept really busy, lately.

Frontius had a small job to do painting Aquilius' office in the Basilica, as he'd realised that it was beginning to look scuffed and needed freshening up, so he'd contacted Frontius. But that wasn't to be done until later this afternoon, after Aquilius had left, having finished his morning's hearings and other duties.

Frontius decided to take the morning off, and wandered down to the seafront to walk along the beach. He frowned and stared at the waves. They seemed to be further away from the shore. He thought that perhaps he was imagining things. It was quiet and still, too eerily still. Something didn't seem quite normal.

He soon became aware, once he paid more attention to his surroundings, that the usual early morning chirping of the birds and barking of dogs had totally stopped. There was a strange, unworldly atmosphere that left him feeling somewhat shaken. Looking up, he was shocked to notice what looked like steam rising from the top of Vesuvius. For a few moments he simply stood and stared.

Suddenly, there was a gigantic, ripping roar and the earth heaved under his feet. Frontius stood absolutely still, frozen with fright. The people of the town were used to minor earth tremors and had also experienced one major event years ago, but this was far worse. He had no idea what was happening now.

He hurried back to his apartment, passing small groups of people standing talking with animation in the streets. Strong earth tremors followed, but residents were uncertain of what action they should take, if any.

Following restless hours that night, the town's residents returned into the streets again just after dawn, where they witnessed Vesuvius erupting, spewing steam and volcanic material high into the sky in the shape of a massive cloud shaped like an umbrella pine. Lightening slashed across the volcano. The new day had brought a sullen sun with a sky a vicious shade of blood red, glowering through the ash and growing darkness.

It wasn't long before it might as well have been midnight, the blackness was so all enveloping.

Many, including Frontius, made the decision to flee the town immediately. Gathering the small amount of coins he'd saved into a pouch and tying a few clothes into a bag, at the last moment he grabbed a couple of his best smaller paint brushes. Then he fled towards the town gate, which was just starting to become crowded with panicked people.

Running, then walking when he ran out of breath, Frontius slipped past most of the groups on the road making their way towards Napoli. Many of them were slowed down by children and the old. The road leading away from Herculaneum was soon choked with travellers, but there were some still in the town who considered that the problem would soon go away, and so they elected to remain.

Up in the villa on the clifftop, Leia stared in dismay at Vesuvius as she heard the noise. She ran out onto the balcony and could see people running in chaos. She had no idea what to do.

There was banging on the front door and she opened it to

Herculaneum: Paradise Lost

admit Silvanus who looked petrified with fear. Slamming the door closed he turned to face her.

'Surely, nothing can hurt us here on the clifftop,' he said hopefully. 'We'll be safe, won't we?'

'I really don't know. Should we leave, do you think?'

'We may be in even more danger down there!' Silvanus pointed to the town where people could be seen running wildly towards the city walls.

'Perhaps,' Leia agreed.

'What about the basement?' he suggested. 'The room where the gold was kept is very strong and the walls are thick. We can hide down there.'

Leia began to fill an amphora of water. Together she and Silvanus gathered up a small amount of food and some comfortable pillows.

'I think we should go now,' she suggested hesitantly. 'I don't want to wait too long.'

'That's the only thing we *can* do,' Silvanus agreed. 'When it's all over, everything will return to normal.' He smiled at her reassuringly.

Together they fled to the basement. There they waited in fear.

'I'll never see the master again,' Leia wept later above the roaring of the eruption, just before the deadly flow from Vesuvius overcame them.

'You love him, I can hear it in your voice,' Silvanus stated gently as he placed his arm around her.

'May the gods help me, I do.'

They died there, huddling together for comfort as they held each other. She would never see Calpurnius again.

The sea was sucked even further away from the beach. It was a strange sight that filled those who saw it with terror.

The sky was once again as dark as night and the cloud above Vesuvius grew so large and heavy, that unable to support its own weight, it caved in upon itself with a mighty roar.

One resident ran screaming through the crowds down the Decumanus Maximus like a mad woman, pushing and shoving to get through the throng of people as she exclaimed, 'we are doomed, the gods are punishing us!'

Cassia's main concern was for her guests. When they approached the reception desk seeking information, she advised all of them to leave the city immediately. Next, she gathered her staff together and addressed them.

'You must leave town or I fear for your safety! Thank you all for your dedication to your duty. All of the guests have gone, now you must do the same.'

When she was sure that the hotel was deserted, she took one more look at the lovely leisure retreat she'd created over many years. Locking the gates behind her, she ran. Her destination was the Temple of Isis. She prayed silently as she fled that the underground basement of the temple would protect her. Reaching it, she banged on the door and was admitted, then entered the cellar with the priests and priestesses.

'Come, Cassia, kneel with me,' the young priestess who had previously befriended her invited, her face still calm and accepting.

'Thank you.'

Before long, the deadly pyroclastic flow reached the temple. Cassia died, her hands joined in supplication to the goddess, a prayer to Isis on her lips.

Vennidius remained with Livia in the House of the Black Saloon. The noise and chaos grew worse and worse.

'We have to go or we'll die!' he begged her.

'Go where?' she answered hysterically. 'This is the end of the world!'

'But we'll have some chance of survival if we leave the town,' Vennidius attempted to reason with her.

'I'm not going. You can run if you wish!'

They sat on the bench together in the pretty garden peristyle, paralysed with fear. It was to be their last, terrible decision, the worst one they had ever made.

Livia refused to leave the villa even to the very end.

Not far away, in the locked room of the Augustales, Spurius screamed out to the few who entered, entreating them to tell him what was happening, yelling to them to let him out. He heard the chaos around him, even though he was unable to see outside the small room in which he was imprisoned.

'Let me out of here, I beg you. I can't get out!'

Everyone ignored him as they had neither the key to his room nor the time to use it.

Spurius threw himself on the bed curled up cringing in terror, as the volcano's pyroclastic surge flowed through the bars on the window and into his room. It enveloped him, boiling his internal organs in seconds.

Of other residents who'd remained in the town, most sought refuge in the boatsheds on the beach. They fled there feeling that it was their best chance of survival, sitting in small groups according to their personal family links. Some, trembling with fear, remained apart a little.

These terrified people represented both the rich and the poor of Herculaneum, male and female, freeborn, freedmen and slaves and the most forlorn of all, the children.

The boat sheds were solid and it was reasonable to think that they'd provide protection. Some of the men stood on the sand outside as lookouts, ready to give warning if fatal danger seemed imminent. Sabina's father, Aquilius, was one of them. But when the end came it was so fast that they died where they stood.

Sadly, the vaulted boat sheds, sturdy as they were against earthquakes, could not stop the flow that erupted from Vesuvius. It poured into and over everything, killing all who sheltered within, instantly. There were few survivors amongst those who had not left before it became too late.

A second boiling pyroclastic surge reached Herculaneum and totally buried it. Not a living soul remained in the town.

22

ROME

The Palatine
The Royal Palace

News of the catastrophe that had befallen Herculaneum reached Titus at the palace, delivered by hard-riding horsemen. The first stragglers who'd left Herculaneum were a motley cascade of humanity, most in a state of terrible trauma, having become aware at least to some degree, of the terrible doom that lay behind and around them.

One glance at Vesuvius was enough.

The darkness and noise were terrifying.

They walked, carrying a variety of items that were as much as they could hold. Some wheeled carts, others were slowed in their escape by the need to assist those who were old, young or ill. The impact on the area of Campania spread beyond the towns of Herculaneum and Pompeii.

Napoli did not escape the impact of the earthquakes, but was fortunate not to endure the full fate of those areas of population that lay closer to the eruption. Some seeking refuge remained permanently in Napoli. Eventually, others made their way to Rome.

One of the actions the Emperor took quickly, was to order messages to be sent to those guests who'd attended the dinner with him, advising that they were to remain where they were until he sent for them. They were not to leave the palace.

Gathered together in one of the reception rooms, Calpurnius, Sabina and Prima waited anxiously wondering why they were being held. No guards were in evidence and the summons to attend, when they'd received it, was given with great courtesy.

'I wouldn't worry too much,' Calpurnius advised. 'We've done nothing wrong, so we've no need to be concerned. All we can do is to wait.'

Eventually Titus appeared, his face grave. 'Please be seated. I regret that I have tragic news for you. Vesuvius has exploded and destroyed Herculaneum and Pompeii. Some did escape, but others died.

At the moment it is too soon to establish who the survivors are. It would be a mistake for any of you to return to either of those places.

They have been utterly devastated and are no long even recognisable. No one left in those places has survived. I have made arrangements for your current rooms here to be available to you. Please remain here. I will inform you as soon as there is any information particularly on the names of those survivors who reach Napoli or Rome. I'm sorry I cannot offer you more information yet.

And now, as you'll understand, I have to leave you. I have much to do.'

Titus strode quickly from the room, leaving his three guests to turn and look at each other in disbelief. Shock held them silent for a few moments and then the impact of the news they'd received hit them hard. All of them had lost loved ones and close friends. Their own lives would never be the same again.

Cletus had been briefed earlier at the barracks by his commanding officer. He was shocked by the news, and wondered if Prima and Calpurnius, especially, were fortunate enough to still be in Rome. He was promised any new information would be given to him as it became known.

Ash from the explosion of Vesuvius fell from the sky onto the city of Rome. Citizens looked upwards in surprise, then reached up to wipe away the grey ash that fell on their faces from the eruption, along with the drizzling rain.

Part V

A New Beginning

23

The Caelian Hill
Two weeks later

It wasn't feasible for Sabina and Calpurnius to remain longer at the palace. Although they had not been asked to leave, courtesy demanded that they do so. They were fortunate in that seeing their predicament, several senators came to them offering more permanent accommodation until they could arrange to fund their own home. It was finally decided that they would temporarily accept the offer of a property belonging to Senator Cornelius Lavinius.

The house, located in the highly acceptable location of the Caelian Hill was empty, and Cornelius was only too happy to know that responsible people would be living there. He took them to view the house, ensuring that they were happy with it, and waved away any suggestion of recompense. Instead, he sent a slave to carry wine and a variety of food to the house the day that Sabina and Calpurnius moved in.

They had just settled in, having set a date in the near future for their marriage, when early one evening, they heard a firm knock at their door.

'I'll get it,' Calpurnius told Sabina, 'it's probably not for us anyway.'

He opened the door only to find himself speechless. The visitor was Alexus. Calpurnius could hardly believe his eyes.

'My friend, my friend! When I heard what had happened, I feared I'd never see you again!' Alexus exclaimed as they embraced.

'How did you ever find us?' Calpurnius asked, totally taken by surprise.

'The palace staff have been most helpful, otherwise it might have taken me much longer.'

They moved further into the house and Alexus met Sabina. She could see the obvious, deep friendship between the two men.

'My dear! What an absolutely terrible time you've endured,' Alexus said, turning to her sympathetically. 'And now, if you'll allow me, I have something for you both. But first, tell me Calpurnius, is everything absolutely beyond saving at your estate in Herculaneum?'

'I'm afraid so, Alexus. I've lost everything, including my sweet slave, Leia, and Silvanus, my loyal caretaker. I have real fears that the town will never rise again. Of course, I still have my villa and statuary works at Baiae. But the Herculaneum villa was a family legacy, a treasure trove of classic art beyond price.'

'Ah. Then, I have a gift for you so you can begin to rebuild.' Excusing himself from the room, Alexus sought out two of his slaves and ordered that the very large and cumbersome item he'd brought with him, be carefully carried inside.

'What on earth is it?' Calpurnius wondered aloud as his eyes roved over the unusual, large object.

'Open it and find out!'

As the statue from Samothrace emerged from its packaging, the expression on Calpurnius' face froze. There was absolute silence.

'You do know what this is, don't you?' Alexus asked, somewhat confused.

'Alexus,' Calpurnius answered softly, 'even you have no idea what you've brought to me.'

Alexus stood perplexed as he watched Calpurnius struggle to retain his emotional composure.

'This incredible statue from Samothrace is a family legend,' Calpurnius continued. 'In the time of Julius Caesar, several men of great importance in Rome, including my ancestor, travelled to Samothrace, having heard tales of the classical treasures that it held.'

Alexus waited.

These Romans were honoured by the priests there by being inducted into a mystery religious cult on the island. They were required to take an oath that they would never divulge the secret of the mysteries they were to be instructed in. My dearest friend, what you have brought me, is the missing statue of victory from the temple at Samothrace.'

'I know a little about Samothrace, but not much and I had no idea of its history, especially in relation to your family,' Alexus stated, shaking his head in wonder. 'I'm so pleased to have found it for you!'

'It's wonderful news,' Sabina smiled as she studied the statue. 'I've never seen anything like it!'

'This gift gives me much pleasure to have been able to offer you,' Alexus continued. 'Now you can start again and rebuild your life.'

'Yes. And we will build up the business in Baiae. There are worse places to live than my villa there,' Calpurnius agreed with a rueful smile. He gently ran his fingers over the beautifully sculpted wings of the statue, a look of sheer pleasure on his face. It was a piece worth a price beyond measure.

'You'll visit us in Baiae before long I hope, Alexus?'

'Travel has been more difficult for me these last few years. I didn't know what I would find when I arrived here searching for you this time, I just prayed that you were still alive and I at least had to try. But, if I am able, I will come to Baiae before long. You know, of course, that you're always welcome to travel to Athens to stay at my beautiful villa there. I can offer you every privacy as my home has a private wing for visitors.'

'Thank you, Alexus, for everything. I'll certainly keep your invitation in mind.'

The remainder of that day was spent in celebration. Alexus' generosity and friendship as well as his skill in the antiquities trade, had brought joy which cut through the grief and despair of the death of Aquilius, Leia and Silvanus and the destruction of the villa at Herculaneum.

A couple of months later, Calpurnius received word that Alexus had been found dead in his sleep. Calpurnius grieved for his old friend. At times, he felt as if he was constantly surrounded by death and could not escape it. He asked himself, would the dying never cease?

24

The Esquiline Hill
Vicus Curvus

It wasn't just *any* house!
 Prima couldn't believe her eyes when the litter deposited her outside the front garden of her future home. It was a large, single-storey villa, built on a sizeable block of land with gardens that had been well tended with flowers and hedges. Recent maintenance work had been completed so that it looked as if it was new. Houses in the rest of the quiet street were of the same quality.

 Prima stepped through the front portico and into a large atrium. Light streamed in from the sky through the opening in the roof. Spacious, with a marble-lined impluvium and mosaic floors, the expensive décor had been completed with a small marble table at the end of the impluvium and wall frescoes with country scenes featuring birds, gardens and peacocks.

Just inside the door, to the right, was a small caretaker's room. A tablinum and triclinium opened off the atrium from where a pretty peristyle garden could be seen, surrounded by a colonnade leading to generously-sized bedrooms. A statue of Pan and an intricate fountain provided spectacular features in the garden.

The main bedroom, which would become Prima's, featured friezes of frolicking cherubs who played hide and seek as well as other games and made wine and music. The room's window looked out over the back garden.

Prima took her time as she slowly inspected the whole house. The kitchen was more than adequate and there was a small bathing area, lavishly decorated with a dolphin mosaic and marble seating.

That she was overwhelmed, would be an understatement. She was grateful to Titus for his generosity, especially as the purse of gold coins he'd given her would be vital to start a new life. She pondered on who the last owner of the house had been.

Prima lifted her face to the sun as she sat. Then, eyes unseeing, she gazed at the flowers in the garden. Since the eruption, she'd retained her composure quite well. Suddenly without warning, tears spilled down her cheeks and she could no longer hold back her sobs.

Her thoughts went to Cassia, who had undoubtedly died in the eruption. Prima knew she'd deserved a better fate than that. Julia Felix had survived, but Prima was unaware of that for some time. She sobbed for herself and for the loss of those who'd been kind to her, and accepted her for the person she was.

Eventually, shaking herself free of the sadness that had overcome her, she made the first of many decisions that would frame her future life. She'd willingly remain in the Emperor's service, as he'd suggested she might, with any assistance she could give to help bring enemies of the Empire to justice. That would bring her income as well as being something she was eager to do.

As Prima sat seeing the joyful blossoms around her through eyes misted with tears, it was as though the sun had broken through. She'd grow more flowers in this lovely garden and sell them for special occasions such as weddings. That would earn her additional coins. Bringing joy to the lives of others she was sure, could also help to erase her grief. She'd live her life well in memory of those who had died.

Most of those who'd known her in her old life were dead. If any who survived from Pompeii or Herculaneum chose to bring up her previous work history now, in Rome, she would not apologise for what she'd had to do in order to survive. She, herself, would never raise the subject. She felt a new energy within her to make something more of herself. From now on, she would work as a respected citizen of Rome and put the past behind her.

The next day Prima went shopping. She'd been told to go to the luxury shops in and around the Forum. She was looking forward to an excursion she'd enjoy to take her mind off recent disasters. She was also determined to be wise with the money she spent.

After searching for what she wanted, she came across a shop in one of the side streets that appeared to be owned by a reputable furniture dealer. Stepping inside, she looked for suitable, basic requirements for her home.

The shop held antiques jumbled together with cheap, sometimes damaged, copies. It was large, with a surprisingly varied amount of stock. Prima arrived just as the owner was unlocking the door for the day.

Inside, she took her time searching for what she required, and found a beautifully crafted small table with claw feet. It was topped with marble and almost hidden behind large, empty money chests with a collection of coin caskets on top of them.

'Do you like it?' the shopkeeper asked her, wiping the dust from its surface.

'Yes. I'll buy it. But I also need a bed.'

'Follow me.' He guided her to the back of the shop where she saw a number of well-made, sturdy beds. Prima pointed to one of those with undamaged slats and it was placed to one side with her table.

Her third and last purchase for the day was a comfortable couch, to which she added a quality folding chair. After some lively discussion as to price, agreement was reached.

'These will be delivered to your house in the morning,' the shopkeeper informed her. Prima left the shop well pleased with her morning's work.

She walked the short distance to the Forum, taking in the vitality and colour around her. Public buildings flaunted their marble facades and steps. The graceful temple of Vesta caught her eye, as well as the senate house and the rostra. The Forum teemed with people at this time of the day. They stood in small groups, some discussing politics. Lawyers hurried by to attend the law courts and beggars lounged by the pillars of the public buildings, warming themselves in the sun as they waited for someone to toss them a coin or two.

Fountains provided much needed coolness, although any relaxation they might have provided was lost in the activities going on everywhere. Prima studied the speakers' rostra which had been graced by many over time including famous Romans.

The noise level was high, worsened by the squealing of chickens flapping their wings as they were removed from their cages and sold by busy vendors, and the calls of sellers spruiking their goods. An occasional litter passed by, curtains closed for privacy, and a few senators could be seen arriving early for a senate session. Others made their way into the temples or headed for the bathhouse nearby.

Prima was intrigued. She'd never been to Rome before and she found herself falling under the spell of its vibrancy and splendour. As an afterthought, she stopped to buy honey from a small shop.

Early the following morning she went out to gather information which would be vital to her success if she went ahead with her plan to sell flowers, especially those for important occasions. At first, she'd thought it best to visit local flower sellers, but doubted that she'd learn enough to be successful, and they would probably not be overjoyed at the thought of competition from her.

Prima needed something better.

She walked slowly up Vicus Apollinis, one of just a few streets actually on the Palatine Hill. Before long, as expected, she was challenged at a guard post.

'Announce your business!' one of the guards demanded.

'My name is Prima. I was a guest of the Emperor very recently and I'd like permission to enter the gardens. I wish to consult one of the gardeners,' she explained.

A guard was sent to the palace to enquire if she was known and if so, if permission could be granted.

Before long he returned.

'She has permission,' he announced, 'but on this occasion, only for the gardens. The Emperor has an audience with an overseas ambassador this morning inside the palace.'

Prima smiled as she was waved forward. 'My thanks for your trouble.'

She wandered the gardens without hindrance enjoying their fragrance and colour. Before long, she saw a gardener tending marigolds. He looked up at her as she approached and stopped his work when she spoke to him.

'Salve, my name is Prima. I'm in need of assistance. I've come to you because these are the most beautiful gardens I've ever seen, and there's no one with more knowledge about growing flowers than the gardeners here. Will you help me please?'

He seemed appreciative of her compliment and also her interest. He was a middle-aged man. His face lit up with a smile at her words.

'I'll help you if I can.'

'I've come to Rome from Herculaneum,' she began.

'I'm sorry,' he frowned. 'You must have suffered greatly. I can't even begin to imagine what people from the town of Herculaneum and Pompeii have been through, but it seems at least you have your safety.'

Prima smiled at him.

'Thank you. But I must begin a new life here in Rome. I'd like to grow flowers to sell as I have a good plot of land behind my home but I don't know where to begin.'

'I must continue my work at the moment,' he told her as he glanced behind him nervously to see if he was being watched. It was obvious that he was concerned about being reprimanded for not giving the gardening his full attention.

'Also,' he continued after a few moments, 'it seems that you need more information than the answer to one question. I'd like to help you, though. I can meet with you early this afternoon when my shift for the day is over. Would that suit you?'

'I'm very grateful,' Prima smiled. 'Where should I wait for you?'

'I'll meet you at the other side of the guard post. Salve.'

'Salve.'

From that day onwards, the gardener, whose name was Linus, became a part of her life. It was a delightful friendship for it seemed that he was as happy being able to share his knowledge and teach Prima, as she was to have his help. His wife had left him and they had no children so he was pleased to spend some of his leisure time in such an enjoyable way.

Together, they planned and cultivated the plot behind her home where they grew the most wonderful flowers, including those that were rare, such as water hyacinths. The days flew by in complete contentment. Prima learned to create arrangements that were much sought after especially by brides, but also by the elite households of Rome.

Her reputation for lovely bouquets and other offerings as well as her discretion, especially on sensitive occasions such as funerals, soon spread.

Prima and Linus could often be seen wandering through the royal gardens and public parks, as well as enjoying wine together at the outside tables of various bars as they sat chatting in the sun.

25

The Subura
An Insula

Frontius inspected the two small rooms that passed for an apartment in the insula in which he stood. It wasn't the first time he'd lived in one, but he'd forgotten how squalid and cramped they were. He could only hope that the place wouldn't burn down. To make matters worse, this was the poorest area of the city and filled with criminals. How he wished he was back in his apartment in Herculaneum with its space and beautiful garden courtyard.

Still, he knew how lucky he'd been to escape from the eruption with his life, and especially to find a ride on a creaking cart driven by an old man who took him as far as Rome's city gate. Seeing Frontius struggling to hurry away from the devastation, he'd stopped and gestured to him to jump onto the cart.

Frontius looked around him. This place had no kitchen or other facilities except on the ground floor, and he was on the second. It would have to do, he was too tired to look any further, and with other survivors straggling into the city, any available accommodation would soon be gone.

Pulling out the two paint brushes he'd snatched before he left Herculaneum, he shook his head. They weren't much, but they were all he had to start a new life, as well as the skill he still possessed in the work he was passionate about.

He had to trust that his painting would keep him alive.

Frontius curled up on the floor hoping there were no rats, his small bag of coins hidden underneath him and quickly fell into a deep sleep.

Early the next morning Frontius left the insula and headed for the Forum. He'd slept well, despite the hard floor beneath him. He went looking for the display of work vacancies that were always located there. Inside the doorway of the building someone was taking applications.

Apparently, Emperor Titus was still looking for artisans to help with the decoration of the large amphitheatre which was complete except for its decoration.

He knocked and the overseer looked up.

'Are you looking for work?'

'Yes. I'm a painter of frescoes,' Frontius replied. He saw interest flicker in the man's eyes.

'Are you experienced?' he enquired.

'Yes, I am. I worked on Emperor Nero's Golden House.'

'Well, you've come to the right place. When can you start?'

'Would the day after tomorrow be acceptable?' Frontius asked, hardly daring to believe that he'd had success so easily.

He was told to report to this location and then he'd be taken to the amphitheatre, given supplies and he could commence painting. He'd be paid regularly each week.

'Thanks, I'm really glad to get the work,' Frontius smiled with relief.

'Not half as pleased as I am to get *you*,' the overseer grinned. 'And I need many more painters or the decoration will never be finished. If you know anyone else, let me know.' He looked down at his list and added the newcomer's name to the others. As he walked to the nearest bar to have a drink, Frontius gave a sigh of relief that at least he could now earn money.

He'd never seen anything like it before.

Frontius stopped and stared. He wondered how was it possible to build such a gigantic structure. He hurried after the supervisor as they approached the site. The noise and activity were overwhelming. Pulleys were no longer hauling building materials up the sides of the huge structure, but now had the delicate task of placing life-sized, graceful statues into the many niches created for them, that were presently empty on the outside exterior of the amphitheatre.

'You've been allocated to one of the entrances that leads inside to the seating. Do you see? There are numbers carved above each entrance. Back here, beside this marker, is where the crowds will line up. Entry is to be free.

Actually, I don't know why, but you're decorating the Emperor's private entryway. Probably, its due to your prior work experience. You must be good!'

Frontius saw the supervisor glance at him with new respect. He just nodded in reply.

On the ground just inside the entry he was to decorate he found all of the paint, brushes and sheets of gilding he could possibly need laid out ready. He set to work, happy to have something productive to keep his mind away from the terror of Herculaneum.

Over the days to come, Frontius concentrated on the detailed work in which he was involved. As time went on, the supervisor walked past without speaking and glanced at the walls. Then, one day, when the painting was almost finished, he stopped and waited until Frontius looked up from his work.

'This is wonderful!'

Against a background of people in a crowd, Frontius had painted the figure of a victorious gladiator, standing over his fallen opponent shown lying in despair in the blood and sand of the arena. Overshadowing everyone stood the magnanimous figure of the Emperor, his gesture indicating that the loser should live. Costly colours of blue and green as well as red and white allowed for a vivid rendering of the scene.

Frontius rose and standing with the supervisor, stepped back to survey his fresco which was nearly finished. He wondered what he would do after this when the work ran out.

'You will always have work here for as long as you need it, or at the royal palace, I would think,' the supervisor assured him, as if he'd read his mind. 'I've never seen anything as brilliant as this in my life before. You have great talent!' He clapped Frontius on the back. 'I'll see you tomorrow. You've worked hard. Go home early. You'll still get paid for the whole day.'

What Frontius did not know was that when everyone else had gone and the amphitheatre was silent, Titus always took a stroll around the work in progress each day, unless he was away from the city, assessing its quality and the stage of completion. He paused in front of Frontius' fresco.

'Who is the painter?' he enquired of the supervisor as he continued to study the painting.

'Frontius,' Caesar.'

'Where is he from?'

'He is a free man. He came here recently from Herculaneum following the eruption of Vesuvius.'

Titus smiled slightly, as he murmured to himself, *so, this is another talented citizen of Herculaneum. It must have been a fortunate place indeed in which to live.*

Aloud, he commented, 'This man's work is brilliant. Give him my personal thanks and also a bonus of three hundred aurei on top of his pay. In return, I want his promise that he'll not leave my employment without my permission. And you'd better get that in writing!'

The next day, when told of the events of the day before with Titus, Frontius couldn't believe his luck, which was surely changing for the better. Immediately, he began looking for somewhere else to live and found a ground floor apartment in a different location, with a mosaic floor, running water and three spacious rooms. It looked out upon the luxuriant gardens of Lucullus noted for their ancient Persian character.

III

Since he'd been here last, Frontius saw little physical change in the city of Rome. There was a new building, perhaps, or renovations being carried out, but that was all.

He was on his way home from the amphitheatre one day, not long after he'd received his gift from the Emperor, when he noticed people gathered around a small group of ragged children standing together just in front of the rostra in the Forum. With a couple of exceptions, they were young, perhaps ten years old or so.

Curiosity got the better of him and he stopped to watch.

One of the legionaries stationed there, stepped away from his three companions and unrolling an official-looking scroll began to read:

By Order of the Emperor

The children here today are survivors of the destruction of Pompeii and Herculaneum. Their parents are either dead or missing. It is proposed, upon receipt of the relevant details from upstanding citizens, to give these unfortunates new homes with those prepared to look after them. Only one child may be taken except in the case of siblings. Those children selected to be here today have all been found to be Roman citizens.

In such a devastating situation, Rome will always do her best to provide refuge.

Titus Caesar

Frontius moved towards the children to look at them more closely. His heart was moved to pity for their plight. Unfortunately for them, he thought, many would be used almost as drudges for work in the homes of the rich people who'd provide for them.

He was lost in thought when he felt a tug on his tunic. He looked down to see a small boy standing there looking up at him.

'Please!' was all he said.

'You need someone with more money than me,' Frontius laughed.

'Please!' the boy repeated. 'Help me!'

The smile faded from the painter's face.

The unfortunate urchin was scrawny and needed food by the look of him. His hair was dark and his facial features pleasant. Frontius assessed him as being about ten years old.

'Where was your home?'

'Pompeii,' he replied, 'near the house where the surgeon lives.'

'And your name?'

'Darius.'

'Why did you choose me?' Frontius asked curiously as he looked down into the boy's anxious face.

'You look kind.'

The old painter's heart melted.

From that moment on, he was always going to take the boy and care for him. He thought for a few moments, but could see no problem with taking him to the amphitheatre to watch him as he worked during the day.

Yes. It just might work.

'Come, Darius.' Taking his hand, Frontius guided the boy forward towards the soldier taking down written details, and gave the necessary information. Then, just as quickly, the deed was done and Frontius had a child to care for.

The boy proved to be quiet by nature and seemed bright. He pointed to the splotches of paint on Frontius' work tunic when he was changing it.

'You paint pictures, don't you?' he asked.

'Yes. Did you have some of those in your house?'

Darius nodded his head vigorously. 'They were in every room,' he told Frontius. 'I liked the colours, especially the red and blue ones.'

Frontius made no attempt to try to gather more information from Darius. Undoubtedly the boy had enough right now to cope with. There would be plenty of time later for that. The initial impression he had, though, was that Darius spoke well, appeared to be bright, and had probably come from a comfortable and perhaps, even a wealthy background.

As the years passed, Frontius was never able to find out more about Darius' prior background, but that was never really an issue. It was the present and the future, not the past, that occupied his thoughts.

There was enough space in Frontius' attractive, new apartment for Darius to have his own bedroom, but the first thing his new "father" did was to take him to the baths where he was bathed and his hair washed by one of the slaves. It was then cut. By necessity, he also had to have a couple of new tunics which Frontius bought for him from one of the less expensive shops on the fringes of the Forum.

By the time all of the necessities had been completed, the boy looked utterly respectable and one could even say, he looked handsome.

Darius had a good appetite. Frontius smiled as he watched the boy devouring a plate of fruit and a pastry with honey drizzled over it. It seemed the only problem was that Frontius was going to have to make more money, as well as allowing additional time to buy extra food so that they didn't run out.

26

The Circus Maximus

It was a perfect day for chariot racing. Sunshine and blue skies always drew a noisy crowd who well and truly enjoyed the entertainment provided by whoever was the patron for the day.

It could be thought that the battle and blood of the gladiators would be the most popular, but it was, instead, the chariot races. Some of the drivers were very wealthy men.

If there was one thing that Cletus felt passionate about, it was his beloved *Blues* chariot racing team. He looked around him as the seats filled. Wooden seating lining the sides of the track held tens of thousands, yet they were almost full. Every time they were burnt down or damaged, they were re-built.

The circus looked picture-perfect.

The opening procession around the interior had already

finished. Cletus glanced across to the royal box situated below the Palatine Hill, just as Emperor Titus and his entourage entered. He doubted that there was anything more Roman than the sight before him and the races that would be held throughout the afternoon. Freemen and slaves were trained as charioteers and some became famous, idolised by the admirers who came to see them. Many of them came from other places, such as Greece.

The dolphins signalling the end of each lap had been polished until they shone. No doubt, the central spina would feature in some of the spills during the afternoon as drivers were pushed forcibly against it or lost control.

Cletus' *Blues* lost that afternoon, but he enjoyed himself nonetheless. As the program came to an end, fights broke out as well as lewd cursing and threats against those who would not, or could not, pay up as a result of their losses.

Cletus left and made his way to the Campus Martius. The horses from the teams stabled there were being led inside and placed into their stalls as he arrived. He ran his hand over the gilded decoration on one of the racing chariots standing empty nearby. He had no delusions about the danger to the chariot drivers, some of whom died or were badly injured, but he envied them the adrenaline rush which must have felt incredible.

'I'm here on the Emperor's business,' he told the boy grooming one of the horses from the *Greens* team. 'I need to have a word with the team manager.'

The boy went to get him and a few minutes later, he appeared from the practice circuit. His manner was both practical and to the point and he was obviously busy.

'I'm Gaius. I'm told you want to speak with me. What do you need to know?'

'First, I'd like to see one of the curse tablets that you've received,' Cletus stated.

'The gods know there's been enough of them. One or two

I wouldn't mind, but there is something going on here I don't like,' the manager added in a monotone. Walking to a nearby bench he picked up a thin lead tablet and returned to hand it to Cletus.

'Here. This is just one example.'

Cletus held it in the palm of his hand and read the message, which could not be misinterpreted:

I command you demon, and demand from you this hour that you torture and kill the horses of the Greens and that you kill in a crash their drivers.

'Is there anything else you can think of as well?' Cletus enquired as he handed back the tablet.'

'Oh, yes. Unless I keep someone constantly on guard pieces of equipment are being stolen. Worse than that, someone is deliberately messing with the chariots to cause them to crash. If a charioteer died, would that mean the culprits could be charged with murder?'

'That would be a very real possibility,' Cletus answered. 'You were right to let us know. We don't, however, want to frighten off this offender. Instead of placing an extra, obvious guard, I want you tonight, to remove all of your men. I'll see to security for a few nights and we'll see if we can draw out this criminal. I really hope that it's just a coincidence that this happens to be the team favoured by the Emperor. Keep to your normal routines until you leave tonight, then return as usual in the morning. It may well be that it will take a few nights before whoever it is falls into our trap.'

Gaius nodded. 'I'm glad of your help. I've been worried about the safety of the drivers. The sooner this is cleared up the better.'

With that the two men parted and Cletus returned to the barracks to make arrangements for a couple of back up men to accompany him each night to hide at the stables. Early that night they placed themselves in strategic locations and then they waited.

On the second night, two men dressed in dark clothing were seen slipping in to where the horses' boxes were and the chariots were stored. As Cletus and his men watched, one began to loosen one of the straps on the chariot while the other tossed another curse tablet on the ground near one of the horses.

'I arrest you in the name of the Emperor!'

The criminals, caught in the act and surrounded by Cletus and his men, surrendered without a fight. They were marched to the palace for interrogation.

Cletus returned to his barracks. More and more he was losing the fervent enthusiasm he'd always had for the type of work he did. Perhaps, he thought, he'd speak to his commanding officer in the morning about other options, and if that didn't work out, he'd have to come up with something else himself.

The following morning Cletus hadn't changed his mind and duly presented himself to the office of the commander, Albinus Labienus.

'Come in, Cletus. Take a seat. Now, what can I do for you?' He looked thoughtful as he listened to what was troubling his best operative.

'I believe you need a change of scene in a different placement,' he suggested when Cletus had finished speaking. 'I can't say I'd be pleased to lose you, but I was once in your position, so I know how you feel. I certainly wouldn't suggest Britannia, I don't know how anyone ever survives the weather and conditions there not to mention the people. May I suggest that you consider transferring to Egypt?'

'Egypt?'

'Yes. As you know, I'm sure, it's had a recent history of turmoil. Finally, the place has begun to settle down, though. You could be very comfortable there and it's a totally different culture. You might even like it! I know they'd be delighted to have you. It's not every day they're offered someone with the Emperor's Order of Valour! Take a couple of days to think about it then let me know.'

It really only took Cletus several minutes to decide that he'd take the offer. He'd never been to Egypt, so it would be a new environment for him.

Cletus knew he'd miss Rome, but he also knew that if he was to remain sharp and successful in what he did for a living, not to mention, alive, he needed a change of scene. Once he'd made up his mind, he was surprised how much he was looking forward to the new posting.

Feeling far more enervated, he informed his commander of his decision two days later. He didn't have to wait long for an acceptance to come through from the Roman Governor of Egypt, Prefect Cassianus Priscus.

27

EGYPT

Alexandria

There was something so sensual and exotic about Cletus' first glimpse of the harbour at Alexandria that it quite took his breath away. He stood on the deck, a slight breeze lightly caressing his hair. There was altogether too much to overpower the senses to be able to immediately process it all. The famous lighthouse stood guarding the entry as waves flung themselves upon the heptastadion causeway that linked it to the mainland.

He stared at Cleopatra's royal palace situated on Antirhodos Island, with its own small harbour and as his ship neared the shoreline of Alexandria, he glanced across at the opulent facades of houses of the wealthy merchants and nobles, some of which still lined the foreshore. Cletus had no doubts about the stunning marble grandeur of Rome, but this city was something quite different and itself, totally spectacular.

At least from where Cletus stood, the Alexandria known to Romans visiting Antony and Cleopatra not too many decades before this day, looked utterly beguiling. So, it seemed that the stories they'd told later, really were true!

The office of the Roman Prefect was located in the back area of the palace. Cletus walked towards it to present his authority to join the security unit. The closer he got the more the immensity and beauty of the palace were overwhelming. Beside it stood a dainty temple to Isis.

The main entry was high and formed from red Aswan granite. Guarding it on the day Cletus arrived were four Roman legionaries, two on either side of the heavy double doors. Upon showing his identification, he was admitted and a world of wonder met his sight.

Everywhere he looked gleamed with marble and he walked on onyx floors. Chairs, couches and tables studded with precious gems welcomed him and a gentle breeze off the sea brought alleviation from the heat. The air was laden with the perfume of lotus flowers. Cletus wondered how much, if any, the palace had changed since Cleopatra had graced it, and asked directions from a legionary to find his way to the office of the commander.

'Be seated!' Cassianus Priscus, Prefect of Egypt, invited him when Cletus entered his study for his pre-arranged interview. 'Welcome to Alexandria. You've been here before?'

'I haven't, sir.'

Priscus smiled and gestured towards the official papyri spread across his desk. 'You'll find things here vastly different from what you're used to in Rome.'

'I suspected that might be the case,' Cletus agreed, 'if my first look at the harbour and palace area is anything to judge by, I was correct.'

'I must say that I'm very pleased you've come,' Priscus

continued. 'Your commander in Rome went to some trouble to impress upon me the quality of your past and present service there and your award from the Emperor.'

'Sir, do I understand correctly that you have under your command a special undercover investigation unit?' Cletus asked.

'Indeed, I have,' Priscus informed him, 'however, it's quite small. Nonetheless, the work done by my operatives is of good quality and very necessary in a place such as this. You'll find many cultural differences here, but I've no doubt that you'll become used to them. You'll soon learn the folly of buying too many colourful but useless items from the markets.'

'I've arranged for one of the unit's members to accompany you on a guided tour of the city tomorrow morning.' He handed instructions to Cletus giving the time and place of meeting.

'My thanks, commander.'

'One piece of advice, Cletus, before you go,' Cassianus Priscus offered as he stood to face him, 'don't let the beauty and extravagance of this place give you a false feeling of security. Alexandria is a dangerous city and many of its officials and people are killers who are often deceptive and corrupt as well. You'll have to feel your way carefully at first.'

Cletus didn't miss the severity of his expression and the warning in his eyes.

'This city is more dangerous than Rome?' he asked, incredulous.

'Certainly,' Priscus confirmed. 'And one of your major problems will be being in an environment that's also new to you, and utterly different from the one you've been used to. Always carry your gladius near to hand. Well, now that I've thoroughly put you off staying here, do you have any further questions?'

'Where am I to have accommodation, sir?'

'In keeping with what I've just told you, your unit is located somewhat unexpectedly, in one of the old merchant houses on the foreshore. This has been chosen mainly for privacy as well as easy access to the palace, the harbour and the army barracks. Do not give out your new address to anyone except someone authorised to have that information.'

'No, sir.'

'Ask one of the legionaries at the door to direct you to your place of accommodation. Dismissed. Enjoy your guided tour tomorrow with Flavius.'

Cletus left the Prefect's office with the decided impression that his request for an interesting change was going to be a little more demanding than he'd expected.

Having been dismissed, Cletus made his way back through the palace doors and along the harbour foreshore. He knocked at the house he was searching for and it was opened by a middle-aged male wearing a plain Roman tunic. He waited for the visitor to speak.

'My name is Cletus,' he said, as he'd been directed.

'Welcome. Please enter,' came the reply.

Cletus followed his guide through a narrow hallway which led past rooms on either side to a reception area and kitchen. The house was clean and relatively neat as well as probably free of any small rodents, due to the large black cat that sat sunning itself near one of the windows. He was to discover that the Egyptians honoured cats for their religious importance.

'I'll show you your bedroom first, then we can talk. I'm Milo. I'm the supervisor of the house and staff.'

'Have you been here long?' Cletus asked.

'It's nearly four years now,' Milo answered pleasantly. 'This one is yours,' he announced as he opened one of the bedroom door partitions. Inside, the room was furnished with the necessities, a bed, side table and a chest for clothes. Curtains hung at the window. They'd been left half open allowing sunlight to flood the room.

Cletus had seen worse rooms in his time, but it certainly

didn't come up to the standard of his prior quarters in the commander's barracks in Rome. There was a quirky feel to the place, though, that he found appealing, at least at the moment.

And it had one major advantage. He could hear and see the ocean, something that wasn't the case in his prior room in Rome. For all its luxury it was far more urban in nature.

'Do you have urgent access to a messenger if you need one?' Cletus enquired.

'Yes. They're very prompt and efficient. I believe Flavius will show you around the city in the morning. You'll meet him when he returns here for dinner this evening. Follow me. We'll eat something in the kitchen which should last you through until tonight's meal.'

The two men returned to the reception area where the cat still slept in the sun. So far, Cletus found the new posting interesting. It wasn't quite what he'd expected, but he was innately aware, that life could become far more demanding, than the rather lethargic outer surface and exotic charm that Alexandria presented to unsuspecting newcomers.

'Are you ready for a walk today?' Flavius grunted. He was a big man and Cletus assumed that he could be aggressive if circumstances required it, but he seemed naturally placid by nature.

'I expect our tour of the city will be more than just interesting,' Cletus replied. 'At least it will give me some idea of what I can expect in any particular location.'

'It's a fascinating place,' Flavius continued, 'and it can cast a spell on people.'

'What kind of spell?'

'It's hard to explain. I'd call it something like being under the influence of a potion or drifting away from reality. By the way, do you know that the other name for Egypt, a very ancient one, is *Kemet*?'

Cletus shook his head.

'It means the black land, named after the rich, black soil along the banks of the Nile.'

Cletus gestured towards an amphitheatre they were passing by. It was well built and classical in style.

'Surely, this has to be Roman?'

'It is. One can rarely have a city ruled by Rome unless they build an amphitheatre of some kind. It was probably somewhat different from that in Rome, especially the new one, not only because it's so much smaller, but also some of the entertainment that's held in it.'

It was built by Caesar,' Flavius continued, the unspoken explanation being -who else could it have been? 'There are many obvious signs of the involvement of Rome in the buildings of Alexandria.'

'And what about the open space over there, is it for public use?' Cletus asked.

'As you've probably guessed, it's the Agora, a Greek public area for speaking or gathering for some purpose,' Flavius told him. 'And now we've come to the Caesarium. This is a temple built by Cleopatra in honour of Julius Caesar.'

Cletus stared at the temple then smiled.

'Except for the Egyptian obelisks at the front I've never seen anything that looks more Roman. By the way, is there anywhere here to buy a cup of wine?'

'We'll get some in the Rhakotis district. I need to take you there, anyway. Just make sure you keep your hand on your money. Pickpockets love this place!'

They entered a narrow alleyway lined with shops of every description. It was noisy and colourful. Vendors called out to attract the attention of anyone passing by, extolling the quality of their merchandise. A strong smell of musk mixed with other perfumes hung in the air.

The shops were full of beautiful silks of vivid colours, lotus bowls, perfume bottles, sheets of papyrus, symbols of the Key of Life and many other goods. Cletus understood now how easy it would be to be robbed here or to be cajoled into buying a fascinating item or two that he didn't really need. Cletus wasn't mean, but he looked after his money carefully.

Nearby, they found a place selling drinks and stopped for a few minutes. They were silent as they quenched their thirst and watched those passing by.

'On the way back, Cletus, I'll take you to the Royal Brucheion district near the palace. It's quiet and civilised especially after being where we are now. Alexandria has a number of Jews who live near that district in their own enclave. Most of them are wealthy and they tend to keep to themselves. Over the decades they don't tend to have been well treated by those in power. If I had to guess, I'd say that they're wary and not likely to want to confide in anyone else, especially us.'

That was something to remember, Cletus thought to himself. It seemed he had a great deal to learn not about enforcement as such, but certainly about local customs.

'Another day, perhaps, we can go out close to the city walls and visit the Christian catacombs. Have you visited those in Rome?'

'No. I can't say I have.'

'Then you'll probably find these unlike anything else you've ever seen before.' Flavius added.

'Thanks for the tour. It's been most interesting and quite entertaining.'

'It's been my pleasure,' Flavius grinned, 'but make no mistake, things can become pretty serious here.'

Flavius' expression became stern. 'Take my advice. Be very careful if you're walking alone, because as in any city the laneways and particularly the darkest streets are the worst. We try whenever possible to travel with another agent. Even though we're not in Roman uniform, these people are smart. They know who we are.

Some are friendly towards Rome and benefit from having us here. There are others, however, who would just as happily cut our throats for us.'

He made a slashing motion across his neck. It was not a pretty sight.

28

After a tiring day, Cletus slept well. He ate breakfast when the sun woke him early the following morning, then, after some casual conversation with the other agents, he returned to his room, relaxing on his bed as he awaited further orders. Hands folded behind his head, he lay there enjoying listening to the relaxing sound of the waves meeting the beach just in front of the house. Soon after, he heard someone tap on his door.

'Intrare.'

Flavius came in holding a folded papyrus sheet for him.

'This has just arrived by messenger,' he said as he handed it over. 'I thought I'd better bring it in immediately as it has the seal of the commander on it.'

'Thanks. Let's see what he has to say.' Cletus sat up and having opened the message, read it with interest. Flavius had been correct. It came from Prefect Cassianus Priscus.

Salve Cletus,

I trust you are becoming acquainted with the city. I make it a practice to have dinner with each newcomer to your particular unit, when they first arrive.

Therefore, I hope you are available to attend at my residence in the royal quarter the day after tomorrow at sunset. The only other person in attendance will be my daughter, Vita.

Please reply as soon as possible by messenger.

Cassianus Priscus
Prefectus Alexandreae et Aegypti

'Is the messenger still here?' Cletus asked Flavius as he quickly wrote a reply.

'Yes. I thought it best to have him wait.'

The message was sent and Cletus turned to Flavius. 'Is there anything I should know before attending that dinner?' he asked with a slight frown.

Flavius shook his head.

'One thing, perhaps. Cassianus is straight-speaking and prefers men who are honest with him. He's actually a good commander who cares about the men. I think you'll enjoy the evening.'

Flavius walked out of the room and Cletus was left to ponder how on earth he was going to make sensible conversation all evening with a man he'd only met before for a few minutes. He didn't want his new posting to be trampled in the dirt so soon after arriving.

He'd think about it. And should he take flowers for the Prefect's daughter? He'd check with Flavius later.

On a balmy Alexandrian evening Cletus walked sedately towards the Prefect's house which was located in the quiet and beautiful precinct adjacent to the royal palace. It was a space for contemplation and leisure and seemed to belong in another place and time from the Alexandria he'd just seen of narrow alleyways, bustle, noise and danger. In his hand he held a bunch of flowers quickly purchased in the market.

Spacious green lawns were soft and lush underfoot, broken only by a small pond filled with lotus flowers floating gently on its surface. The sound of the sea was never far away. On approaching the Prefect's house which stood in splendid isolation, he was challenged by Roman guards.

'State your business here!'

They stepped away and allowed him to pass, having been shown the invitation he carried with him. The door was opened to his knock by an Egyptian servant who bowed to him then held the door open for him to pass through.

Cassianus Priscus advanced down the hallway to meet him, his hand extended. He was casually dressed and appeared relaxed as he smiled at Cletus.

'Welcome. Come in and join us for a drink before we dine,' he invited.

'Thank you, sir.'

The house was large and well maintained It passed through Cletus' mind that it must be interesting for Cassianus to be spending his days in the royal palace in the height of luxury, then returning here. Still, the house appeared comfortable and rather homely, which Cletus preferred. Aromas from dinner being prepared wafted through the reception room, where he was offered a seat on one of the couches and wine in a beautifully decorated silver cup. He looked up to see a young woman enter the room and immediately stood up to be introduced to her.

'This is my daughter, Vita,' Cassianus announced. He turned to her, 'Vita, I'd like you to meet Cletus, one of my most valuable agents.'

Cletus was surprised, to say the least and almost speechless as well. She was young and very attractive and advanced towards him, her head slightly bowed in greeting.

'It's a pleasure to welcome you here,' Vita uttered in a quiet, melodious voice. She wore a long Roman robe made of expensive blue silk, and sandals made from fine leather on her feet. Her long hair, caught up at the back of her neck in a net, was dark and her eyes, green. She wasn't very tall. A smile that hinted at mischief played easily upon her lips.

'Shall we go in to dinner before we all starve?' Cassianus laughed. Cletus thought that no doubt he was used to having men speechless when any of them first met Vita. It wasn't as if there were many Roman women, especially one so lovely in Alexandria for the men in military units to mingle with.

Later, Cletus would raise with Flavius the matter of why he'd not been warned to expect the sight of this young woman. No doubt, it was a trick played upon every new agent on his arrival when he first visited the home of the Prefect. Flavius merely laughed.

Cletus enjoyed the evening far more than he'd anticipated. Good food and wine arranged on a beautifully set table as well as laughter and many tales of Cleopatra and Antony flowed during dinner.

The ambience was soothing.

As the evening wore on, Vita excused herself and retired, leaving her father and Cletus alone. They discussed politics and most of all, in some detail, past and present events in Alexandria.

The two men related very easily to each other. Cletus had no doubt that Cassianus had every reason, moving forward, to be concerned about the state of affairs in Egypt, especially in Alexandria.

Rome could not afford to have a failing economy here. Its people relied considerably on good harvests of grain to supply them with grain. One of the worst situations any emperor could be faced with was a shortage of bread. Failure of the

Nile River to flood was far from an uncommon event. When that happened, not only the population of Egypt went hungry.

The shadows of the doomed lovers, Antony and Cleopatra and their gruesome deaths still hung over the city of Alexandria, as did an inherent unease that spoke of the possibility of future riots and murders against Roman rule.

'Would you have time to escort me through the gardens?'

Cletus turned a few days later to find Vita with a maid accompanying her in one of the better markets.

A praetorian guard stood back behind them.

'What a pleasant surprise,' he said in greeting, responding to her question and gentle tap on his shoulder. 'I'm sorry, Vita, I didn't realise you were standing there. Certainly, I'd be delighted to accompany you.'

Flavius, who'd been with him made his excuses and left them as did the guard. He hurried away with Vita's maid and they magically disappeared in the direction of the palace.

Cletus took Vita's arm and they turned towards the royal gardens and the harbour. He found her voice melodic and attractive.

'Do you like Alexandria?' Cletus asked.

'I do, but I'm not sure I could live here forever.'

'How long have you been here now?' he enquired politely.

'I believe it's around three years. Time does pass quickly,' she smiled.

They walked along the foreshore and on to the royal gardens, in pleasant conversation. Cletus decided to find out more from her about her background.

'Are you not lonely here with so little female company?' he queried.

'Not really,' she replied. 'I do miss shopping in Rome,

though. As you've probably noticed, it's quite different here and I also need to be careful. My father is very stern about my security.'

'How much longer do you think your father will be at this posting?'

'We don't know yet. As long as things remain fairly calm politically it's possible Rome may leave him here for some time. It's really difficult to predict.'

As a few weeks went by they met again, occasionally, and sat talking in the gardens beside the lotus pool. It was surprisingly quiet and restful. There was a natural attraction between them and they enjoyed their time together, but Cletus was far from seriously involved.

29

One morning not long after, Cletus was surprised to receive an order to attend at the Prefect's office within the hour. It seemed unusual and he wondered what had caused Prefect Cassianus to send for him. He presented himself within the given time and was ushered into his office. It wasn't Cassianus, however, who was waiting for him, but the Prefect's second-in-command.

'I've been told to give you these documents,' he began, handing them over to Cletus. 'You have been posted back to Rome and will depart on the next ship. It leaves tomorrow. You are to report to your commanding officer when you arrive.'

Cletus was speechless. Silently, he looked from the documents to the Legate standing in front of him, waiting for an explanation, but none was forthcoming. He strode from the office puzzled at what had just occurred.

'It's very strange,' Flavius commented when Cletus

described what had happened. 'I've never heard of a situation like this before. We'll all be sorry to see you go.'

They shook hands.

The next day Cletus took one final look at Alexandria as his ship departed the harbour. His future was unknown. Arriving safely back in Rome, he remained bewildered at reasons for his unexpected, hasty exit from Egypt.

'Come in, Cletus!' Commander Labienus came forward to shake his hand. 'I must say, I'm not sorry to have you back again, the place has been absolute chaos since you left. Please take a seat.'

Cletus sat warily waiting for, he didn't know what.

'I've received a report from the Prefect in Alexandria,' Commander Labienus began.

He paused.

Cletus gripped the sides of his chair.

'He's left it to me as to whether I devise some story to tell you that might explain your quick exit from Alexandria, or whether I tell you the truth.' He glanced up and his eyes met those of his agent.

Not good. Not good at all, Cletus thought as he waited, not realising that he was holding his breath.

'I respect you and the past work you've done so well for me, too much to lie to you. So, here are the facts.' Labienus paused.

'During the short time you served in Alexandria, you met the Prefect's daughter, Vita, I believe.'

'I did,' Cletus agreed.

'The Prefect does not accuse you of any wrongdoing,' Labienus continued, 'but his daughter was seen as becoming too fond of you. He says you were probably not aware of the fact that he'd already agreed, unofficially, to a betrothal between Vita and his second-in-command. Vita is not exactly happy with this proposal. You were ordered to leave in order to clear the path for the betrothal to take effect as smoothly as possible. Had you stayed, Vita would, undoubtedly, have been even more difficult to control.'

There was a brief silence.

'He could have just told me never to see her again,' Cletus suggested, somewhat irritated.

'Perhaps. But my understanding of this young woman is that she is extremely stubborn,' Labienus explained. 'Anyway, it's not so bad to be back is it?'

'That's true,' Cletus agreed. 'But what about my service record?'

'The Prefect has promised that there will be absolutely no blemish on it,' Labienus stated reassuringly. 'I give you my word that I will check that myself, however, to make sure that it's true.'

'I must say, I'll be happy back in Rome,' Cletus admitted.

'How about your old room back?' Labienus grinned. 'Just like old times!'

'That sounds fine to me.'

'You have three day's leave, then you begin work here again.'

The two shook hands and Cletus settled back into his usual role. With the death of Commander Labienus from a fever three years later, Cletus was promoted by the Emperor to the vacant position of Commander of the barracks.

30

ROME

The Esquiline Hill
Villa of Scribonius Amerinus

The young couple were so much in love that they had eyes only for each other. The gracious home in which they stood, captivated all who were fortunate enough to have received an invitation to attend a wedding in one of the most elegant houses in Rome. Early morning showers had passed leaving in their wake a mild and warm day. The formalities having been completed guests mingled happily as they enjoyed the delicacies laid out for their pleasure.

'My name is Scribonius Amerinus. Have we met before?' Prima looked up to see a smiling senator gazing down at her.

'I don't believe so,' she replied, returning his smile.

'You're a friend of another guest then?'

'No. I provided the freshly cut flowers for the house for this occasion and the floral arrangements,' she explained, 'and the couple kindly suggested that I stay.'

'I must compliment you. I find the flowers glorious. You are obviously very talented.'

'Thank you for your compliment. It's been a lovely wedding. I'm Prima,' she responded.

They were joined by a friend of Scribonius. 'Am I interrupting anything?'

'No, certainly not, 'Scribonius assured him. 'I was just admiring the flower arrangements that this young woman supplied for the wedding. May I introduce you to Prima?'

'It's a pleasure,' my dear. My name is Matidius Patrunius. Would you like another cup of wine?'

'Yes, please.'

Both men were middle-aged and wore the purple stripe of senators. Prima found them pleasant and unassuming, their manner and speech highly cultured. They spoke for a short time then drifted apart.

Prima was exhilarated to be in the company of guests considered the elite of Rome, and this was not the first time it had occurred. She hadn't thought about the social implications when planning to pursue her work with flowers, but it was paying dividends not only with her income but also her enjoyment of meeting new people.

A few days later, after this most recent wedding, she opened her door to a messenger. He waited for her answer.

Salve Prima,

I enjoyed our meeting at the wedding. Would you consider having dinner with me at my home? Several guests will also be attending. Your company would surely add to the pleasure of our evening.

If you are in agreement, please advise the messenger and I will send a litter for you that night. The dinner will be at sunset next Thursday. I look forward to seeing you then.

Senator Matidius Patrunius.

Having replied in the affirmative, Prima decided that she needed to shop for such an occasion to buy something more appropriate than she already owned. She was surprised and pleased by the invitation. It was one more step on the ladder to the new life she sought to lead.

She went shopping and enjoyed herself immensely. She had enough coins to buy exactly what she wanted, and she did. Prima was a stunning looking woman and she was very determined to match or excel any other women at the dinner regardless of their social class.

The litter came for her, as arranged, just before sunset on the following Thursday. Settling herself in comfort Prima sat back relaxed, drew the curtains for privacy, and contemplated the evening ahead. The house of Matidius wasn't far away, on Vicus Fanni on the Aventine. They arrived quickly at their destination.

Matidius came to the door to personally escort her inside. 'You look absolutely incredible. How beautiful you are,' he complimented her.

'The lady is, indeed,' Scribonius commented as he came towards them. Prima was pleased that there was one guest at least, that she'd already met before, even if only briefly.

There were only two other guests that night at dinner. One was Julia, the sister of Matidius. A middle-aged woman whose looks were fading but who must once have been beautiful came to greet her. Prima liked her immediately. She had great charm and grace and did her best to put their guest at ease.

'How wonderful that you've been able to join us tonight,' she told Prima. 'It can become so boring when only men are here and tell their political stories. Come and join me.'

They sat in comfort on one of the oversized couches and Julia drew Prima into conversation with the ease of a woman who is socially experienced. They'd just begun to discuss the trivial information that usually preceded more major revelations, when dinner was served.

The evening was a great success for Prima. It hadn't taken long before she was laughing and enjoying herself. She liked the people she met and just hoped that none of them would probe too deeply into her past. She'd revealed that she'd escaped from the eruption of Vesuvius, but nothing more about the work she did there. Those present were shocked that she'd endured such a terrible event and plied her with sympathy.

'My dear Prima,' Julia said as she was about to enter her litter to leave. 'It must be difficult for you being new to Rome. I shall make sure that we give you every assistance to settle into your new home.'

Matidius had lost his wife many years before to one of the many plagues that swept through Rome from time to time. He'd felt that his heart would break but over the years it had healed and revived his interest in social pursuits. He was not an impulsive man who would rush into an inappropriate relationship, however, he felt that he'd like to find again the warmth, caring and companionship that he'd had in his first marriage.

He fell completely under Prima's spell. It had happened quickly and without thought, but as he watched Julia and Prima the night of the dinner, he determined to get to know her better, if she'd allow it.

There was something about Prima. She seemed strong and resilient, but there was a softness and vulnerability as well that strongly attracted him. Matidius decided to discover if they were, in fact, compatible and if she'd be interested in a closer relationship.

It was an exciting time in the weeks and months that followed, as Prima and Matidius enjoyed visiting the various places of interest and beauty in Rome. They watched the performance of a play at the Theatre of Marcellus and went shopping in the Forum and the galleries. They also accepted invitations to visit several of Matidius' friends, who'd expressed a wish to meet her.

One of his closest friends came from the port city of Ostia, south of Rome. Arm in arm, Prima and Matidius called in to his house to see him. Afterwards, they walked the streets of the town enjoying the hustle and bustle of the busy merchant centre. They passed by the small gem of a theatre with its grotesque masks and visited the apartment that Matidius owned, located in the best part of town. He currently rented it out and the tenant happily showed them around inside.

'It pays to have more houses and villas than just where one lives,' Matidius explained to Prima. 'I actually own others as well as this one here. I find that it provides me with financial security.'

Prima smiled encouragingly at him.

'I've really enjoyed myself today,' she informed him happily. 'I've also learned much from you.'

Matidius patted her hand.

They walked across the Ponte Cestio bridge in Rome the next day and sat on Tiber Island, in the middle of the fast-flowing river, on a peaceful Roman afternoon. Their arms were linked together. The evening before, Matidius had gently kissed Prima as she left his house to return home after an evening dining with him.

As they sat watching the river and enjoying the daylight fast fading into the approach of night, Prima's expression was serious as she turned to face Matidius. She'd been aware for some time that he was almost certainly in love with her.

'Matidius, there is something I must tell you. You don't yet know very much about me or who I was in my life before I came to Rome.'

He raised an eyebrow and gestured to her to continue.

'I wasn't always the person I am now,' she began slowly. 'I was poor when I arrived in Pompeii on my own and had to find a way to earn enough to live on. I was…'

Before she could continue, Matidius reached across and gently placed his finger over her lips.

'I already know,' he murmured.

Prima's expression was one of complete surprise and consternation. She sat frozen, unable to speak.

'Do not trouble yourself over it,' Matidius continued. 'I do not need to hear you say more, although your honesty does you great credit. I'm a Roman Senator, which means I not only have wealth but I also carry a responsibility to present myself with a certain amount of dignity. I had your background checked out long ago.'

Tears came to Prima's eyes and she turned her head away. Matidius drew her close to him and gently turned her face back towards him.

'Please forgive me for looking into your life. It isn't because I have doubts about us. Your past is just that and I know you as you are now, so I will trust my own judgement. But, Prima, the day may come when I will need to protect you.

There are some in this city who would use blackmail against you if they came to know your past social class. It's fortunate that the sad devastation by Vesuvius buried not only the cities of Pompeii and Herculaneum, but also removed almost everyone who knew about your past life.'

'You're not angry?' Prima whispered.

'No. Why should I be?'

'I wouldn't blame you if you were.'

'You did what you had to do to survive. That is not a crime.'

Matidius took Prima's hands in his and smiled at her. He looked into her eyes. 'Will you marry me?'

'Yes. With all my heart.'

Matidius kissed her tenderly and held her in his arms. 'Then, we will move on together,' he murmured. 'I believe we have great happiness to look forward to in the years to come!'

All of the tension and stressful years behind Prima melted away as she and Matidius walked back across the bridge and into a new future together.

31

The Amphitheatre

Finally, the Flavian Amphitheatre was finished! It proved as decade followed decade, to be a theatre of death and pain where the spilling of human blood was commonplace and expected. For those who lived at the time it was, without question, a miraculous place of excitement and entertainment.

A few days before the opening, Frontius had put the finishing touches to the wall decorations. He'd been given the job of final touch-ups and checking on the other fresco painters' work, and told to make changes as he saw necessary. His new son, Darius, sat quietly watching him as he painted.

And then it was complete.

The supervisor, in final thanks, spoke to Frontius on his last day at the site. 'Here are numbered clay tablets for entry on the opening day and an additional invitation tablet as well. All tickets are free, but at least you won't have to stand in line waiting for entry.'

Darius was so excited he chattered on about it for days beforehand. When the day finally arrived, he carried with him his toy sword.

If a hint of sadness hung over the opening due to the earlier death of Vespasian, it was quickly dispelled. Citizens found themselves waking to a glorious Roman day and there was a real buzz in the air.

The new amphitheatre was already a hive of activity, not seen by those waiting to enter. Underneath the arena surface, people tasked with making the magic happen were scurrying along in darkness carrying out their work with the help of flares.

The noise level rose substantially with the arrival of the wild animals and their keepers. The gladiators were also arriving under the control of the various lanisters. Their fighting helmets and equipment were laid out on long tables for easy collection when the moment for their appearance in the arena arrived.

A system of winches and ramps were ready to lift both animals and gladiators, unseen, to the arena surface where they would suddenly appear from trapdoors to roars of delight from the thousands waiting. The generous distribution of gifts of coins and bread to the crowd beforehand added immensely to their excitement.

Before entering, Frontius and Darius stopped outside to watch the scene around them. Frontius was happy to note how many of those in the crowd pointed to the frescoes, admiring the workmanship and creativity he and fellow artisans had achieved.

'Move along! Move along!' Ushers hustled the crowd towards the entry arches.

Frontius and his son showed their priority authority and

walked freely through to their seats, climbing stairs of marble. As dictated by social class, they were a long way up from the arena but the amphitheatre was so well designed that they still enjoyed a good view.

The musicians set themselves up ready to play and it wasn't long before the acrobats made their appearance. Dressed in colourful clothing and carrying tiny swords and other make-believe weapons, they cavorted around the arena playing jokes on each other, some of them crude, and doing tumbling tricks.

Then came an assortment of wild animals. Most people had never seen anything like the panthers, lions and other creatures captured in the far corners of the Empire and sent in cages to Rome.

Darius was captivated.

The entry of Emperor Titus was met by thunderous applause. He was popular with the people, understandably, given the money he'd spent to provide such unbelievable entertainment. After the luncheon break, when the people had enjoyed eating the nuts, oysters or other enjoyable treats, the afternoon program began and the arena initially grew a little quieter in the expectation of what was to come.

A couple of Bestiarii appeared. Trained to fight wild beasts they fought often against the lions. The crowd began to roar. It was mainly the animals who were killed that first afternoon, but that wasn't always the way such a bout finished.

The noise of the audience mingled with their sweat as they sat cheering in the heat. They awaited the next event in anticipation. Convicted criminals were forced to enter the arena and the lions were let loose.

Some were crucified.

A few were not criminals but Christians, most of whom died at the Circus Maximus or on Vatican Hill.

Soon the sand of the arena floor was saturated with blood and their agonised screams rang out across the amphitheatre.

The highlight of any afternoon's entertainment, however,

was the next event. Bouts of single combat took place featuring trained gladiators who were matched in pairs against each other. Nearly all were slaves, however, some were free citizens attempting to earn enough coins, usually to pay back debts owing to money lenders.

Roman matrons made no secret of their admiration for the physically athletic appearance of the gladiators. Many sexual relations occurred, instigated by the upper-class wealthy women of the city.

Many lives were lost due to the Emperor's decisions before the end of that day. Trained to die with acceptance in order to maintain respect, each beaten gladiator condemned to die did so with submission, once their raised arm requesting life had been answered with a death decision from the Emperor.

Combat on this occasion was *to the death*.

They were carried out of the arena through the Gate of Death. Those who were most popular with the crowd and therefore more likely to be allowed to live, departed through the Gate of Life to fight another day.

More than a few gladiators were injured, some badly, and in the allocated room under the amphitheatre, physicians worked to treat them and try to alleviate their pain with potions made from poppies. The skill of the surgeons saved many gladiators' lives, sometimes they were even able to fight again.

At the end of each long day's entertainment Rome's citizens went home happy and excited, and if they were fortunate, carrying whatever gift from the Emperor they had managed to get their hands on.

Frontius and Darius were no exception.

The love of the people of Rome for the amphitheatre's entertainment didn't diminish and was still strong for many decades following the one hundred days that the opening games were held. It was as late as the year four hundred and ten before Rome's people finally lost the games held in their theatre of death. The spectacle of that day, and the

Herculaneum: Paradise Lost

thunderous applause ringing in their ears, remained forever in the memories of those fortunate enough to have been present.

On the completion of the amphitheatre, Frontius had received notice to arrive for work at the new bathhouse also being built by the Emperor over the top of the previous, huge complex known as Nero's Golden House. He was given ongoing work until it was completed and then he painted frescoed walls in the royal palace.

In recognition of his service Frontius received a pension which enabled him to remain in his apartment for the remainder of his life. Darius attended school and became highly proficient in Greek and mathematics. He was a good student, serious by nature, who caused no worry for his father as he grew taller and stronger.

Although Frontius attempted to teach Darius to paint frescoes, he proved to his father's disappointment, to have no particular talent for it. He was later to become one of Rome's great engineers.

Darius was grief stricken when Frontius died nine years after he'd first reached Rome following the destruction of Herculaneum. By then, his father was a frail, old man looked after by his adopted son.

In his final days, the old painter told anyone who would listen, that the years spent with his new son had been by far the most happy of his life. He often thanked the goddess, Fortuna, for turning his steps towards the group of children that day, when he was allocated Darius to care for.

Frontius' funeral was attended by the supervisor who'd worked with him at the amphitheatre.

'This man was special, very much so!' he told those attending. 'I was amazed by his incredible talent. He certainly was a master fresco painter. Frontius came to us from Herculaneum.

He was a humble person without arrogance. I consider myself honoured to have known such a man.'

The frescoes Frontius painted to decorate the great amphitheatre, were still to be seen on its walls in the many centuries that followed.

32

BAIAE

There were no words to describe the glory of Baiae! Calpurnius glanced across at Sabina, an amused expression on his face. She was completely immersed in the scene in front of her as they arrived at the luxury seaside resort. Her wonder heightened further as they came to the Piso villa, and she gazed in disbelief at its location and size.

'I can't believe this place,' Sabina exclaimed, unable to conceal her excitement, not that she really thought that she needed to. 'I had no idea that this place would be so…so incredible!'

Calpurnius laughed. It pleased him to see Sabina's face free of grief for the first time since her father's death.

'There's something I must do before we continue to look around.' After searching through their belongings, he found what he was looking for. The wonderful fresco by Fabullus, given to him by the Emperor was soon gracing the wall in the room in which they stood.

'How wonderful!' Sabina exclaimed. 'We'll keep that forever.'

'See that villa beside us a little higher up the clifftop?' Calpurnius gestured to Sabina, 'that's the imperial villa.'

She looked up at it curiously.

'I'm told that Titus doesn't use it, so it remains empty. Interesting, isn't it, how two emperors can be so different from each other.'

'Are we allowed to look around the outside of it?' Sabina enquired hopefully.

'I don't think there would be a problem,' Calpurnius answered, 'unless we try to actually enter the inside. Let's walk up there.'

Arm in arm they climbed up then walked across to the imperial estate. Calpurnius had been correct. The villa lay empty and silent. Walking into the front garden, they stood surveying the view, which was spectacular.

'It seems a pity that all of this is wasted,' Sabina commented thoughtfully. 'I wonder how long that will be the case?'

Calpurnius looked around but could see no one other than themselves. 'That question is not one to ask in public,' he replied, 'but just between us, not long I don't think. The new emperor after Titus is likely to be his brother, Domitian, and he will be very much a different type of ruler. If I had to guess, I'd say that we should make the most of our days under Titus while we can.'

That afternoon they walked together on the beach. They were to marry once they'd settled into their villa. For Sabina, this time was one of wonder and healing. For Calpurnius, it was a time to look to the future.

Later that day they visited the statuary workshop. Business was still brisk and the profits large. He knew that he'd need every coin it earned to rebuild his assets after the huge losses at Herculaneum.

Calpurnius still had recurring dreams about the horrors of the eruption, even though he'd been physically absent at the time. A few days after it occurred, he'd made a promise to himself, one he meant to keep.

He spoke to Sabina just after they'd arrived at the villa. 'If I arrange for attendants and a guard to be here with you while I'm gone, would you mind terribly if I return to Herculaneum?' He watched to see her reaction. 'I'll only be away for a short time,' he added.

Sabina looked up at him, surprised.

'Why are you going back to Herculaneum?'

'To say goodbye to your father, Leia, Silvanus and the other people I knew. Sabina, I must find closure if I'm to go forward without the sadness that haunts me. Please don't ask if you can come with me. I don't think it's something you should have to endure.'

Sabina nodded her acceptance of his decision.

'I understand. Of course, you should go. I fear, though, that it may break your heart if you look for your family villa there.'

'You may well be right but I must do this.'

EPILOGUE

80 A.D.

The day was cool and the air crisp when Calpurnius departed from his villa in Baiae. He rode at a moderate pace, dreading what was yet to come.

Napoli had escaped any real damage and was functioning as usual when Calpurnius arrived. In the early evening he walked along the foreshore of the city's perfect bay, the jewel for which the city was famous and allowed his mind to roam back through the years, remembering events of note in Herculaneum and also ordinary days memorable only for their warmth and serenity.

He tried to ready himself for the following visit but soon realised that such a thing was impossible. His overnight stay could not prepare him for the reality of the situation, but at least the upcoming ordeal would soon be over.

The next morning, Calpurnius rode for Herculaneum.

As the sun sank below the horizon and the light began to dim, he reached the dead city. There was no path for entry through what had once been the city walls.

Except for part of a few of the very highest walls, the city had simply disappeared. What remained was a version of hell. Herculaneum was entirely devoid of any colour, except one.

Black. Everywhere.

It was no longer possible to see roads or where individual buildings and houses had stood. Only irregular bumps and lumps of varying shapes and sizes remained, all covered by the noxious lava vomited out by the volcano.

The tall palm trees were gone.

Calpurnius strained his eyes and eventually saw an unrecognisable volcanic mass where his villa had once stood. He bowed his head paying homage to Leia and Silvanus, to Aquilius and the others claimed by the fury of Vesuvius.

With the help of Sabina, he would go on.

There would be another Calpurnius Piso to follow him. The child would become a man who'd build the future.

The exquisite winged statue Alexis had given him and the utterly beautiful one sculpted by Decius, which had arrived just before the eruption of Vesuvius, were now safe in the Baiae statuary workshop. They remained to him as real financial security and as a memory of other priceless, lost art and manuscripts.

Calpurnius turned his horse around and after a final glance and a whispered farewell, he left Herculaneum forever.

A NOTE ON HERCULANEUM

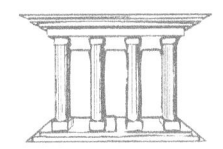

Following the eruption of Vesuvius, the devastated town of Herculaneum entered a period of deep sleep and was all but forgotten by time. Slowly it disappeared from human memory, its treasures buried from sight, its name erased from maps.

The modern town of Resina rose to cover the ruins of the dead town. It included a monastery. One day, while sinking a well in the monks' garden, a workman broke through into the remains of the large, buried theatre in the dead city.

Today, Herculaneum is crowded with visitors, keen to experience life as it was in the town so long ago. The preservation and conservation are unbelievable. It looks as if people simply stopped whatever they were doing and fled, which is, of course, what many of them did.

There have been other eruptions of Vesuvius since that day in 79 A.D. Those who are fortunate enough to explore the town now, rescued by passionate, hard-working archaeologists, cannot help but recognise its value to humanity. We owe them so much for what they have given back to us.

One day Vesuvius will almost certainly erupt again. We can only hope that Herculaneum and Pompeii will be spared any future destruction.

THE AUTHOR

Lorraine Blundell (Parsons) was born in Brisbane, Australia. She lives in Melbourne and has a daughter, Jenni, and a son, Steve. Lorraine graduated from the University of Queensland with a Bachelor of Arts Degree majoring in English and History. She holds a teaching qualification in Drama from Trinity College, London.

She trained as a classical singer at the Queensland State Conservatorium of Music, Brisbane. During that period, she sang professionally on television as a solo vocalist, regularly performing for six years on channels BTQ7 and QTQ9 Brisbane as well as nationally on HSV7 Melbourne.

Lorraine is an experienced performer in musical theatre productions. Her interests are singing, ancient history and archaeology.

HISTORICAL NOTES

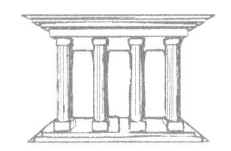

Herculaneum was destroyed by the eruption of Vesuvius in the year 79 A.D. Over recent years, there has been much discussion amongst historians as to the exact time of year that the eruption took place.

August was the accepted month, before ongoing excavations uncovered types of food and plants more in keeping with a later season, and more recently, a graffito just excavated, with the date 17th October 79 A.D. Consequently, that is the month I consider to be most likely to be correct.

Herculaneum and Pompeii were quite different places, and their people died differently. Ash and pumice as well as falling roofs killed victims in Pompeii. In Herculaneum, deaths largely occurred due to boiling pyroclastic flows that enveloped them, literally boiling the insides of their bodies. Residents in the latter city had more time to decide whether to leave before the deadly flows reached them and time ran out.

Death after that time was instantaneous.

Herculaneum was a sleepy, seaside town visited by many seeking a quiet holiday. Wealthy and well organised, daily life for residents would have been usually peaceful and uneventful. Pompeii was larger, brash, bustling, noisy and largely commercial as well as residential.

Nonetheless, Herculaneum seems to have enjoyed all the amenities to be expected somewhere with a larger population. A chariot racing stadium or an amphitheatre has not yet been found, but perhaps one lies buried under the modern city of Resina above. But, a stand-alone theatre, bathhouses, basilica and curia have all been found, as well as a palaestra.

In Herculaneum there were tall palm trees. These are not evident in Pompeii, instead, umbrella pines dominate the skyline. The latter city seems to have had an inferior water management system to handle flooding in the streets – thus, the large, chunky stepping stones for keeping one's feet dry while crossing. The visitor today will find chariot wheel ruts in Pompeii streets but not in Herculaneum due to different street paving stones.

Because they were destroyed differently, the ruins are different. Herculaneum has many second storey buildings still able to be appreciated, even if the upper ones are open to the sky. By contrast most of the top storeys in Pompeii have been destroyed.

On the fringe of Herculaneum was one of the largest, most luxurious, and certainly wealthy villas in Campania. The Villa dei Papyri faced the ocean. The grounds and villa were vast and filled with artistic treasures.

Unfortunately, only a very small part of the villa has so far been excavated. It is enough, however, to indicate that the interior was gorgeous, with colourful wall frescoes and incredible mosaic floors, as well as statues and busts that stood complimenting delightful pools and interior rooms.

When the remainder of the villa will be excavated is unknown. This is due to financial and conservation issues.

The Piso family is very likely to have owned the villa which is thought to have been built by the father-in-law of Julius Caesar. It would probably have passed down the years in family hands until the time of its destruction.

The Piso Villa is famous for the many carbonised scrolls found by excavators in its library. The contents seem to be philosophical in nature or poetry. Scientists are undertaking the difficult task of making them legible again without destroying them.

A branch of the Piso family also owned a magnificent villa in the elite seaside resort of Baiae, north of Naples. It is unfortunate that all of that town can no longer be seen except by underwater diving, a large piece of it having fallen into the sea. It was the seaside home of the royal and elite of Rome.

The winged victory (Nike) statue of Samothrace, from the Greek Island of Samothrace, overlooked the temple of the gods. It was visited by one of the Piso family, together with a few other Romans of great importance in the time of Julius Caesar. They were inducted into the mysteries of the temple which was considered a great honour.

The character, Prima, in the novel is based on the courtesan, Primigenia, who came from Nuceria and visited or lived in Pompeii and Herculaneum. She was praised for her beauty in many scribbled messages written in haste on walls in both places. Whether she escaped death during the eruption of Vesuvius is unknown.

Archaeologists discovered, in the Augustales, a small, locked room with a barred window in which lay a man curled up on the bed. At this time there is no knowledge of who this person was or why he appears to have been imprisoned at the time of the eruption.

It has been suggested that the victim was the caretaker of the building. This seems unlikely, however, as the window was barred and the room apparently locked from the outside.

The huge port of Rome, *Portus*, was built by the Emperor Claudius largely due to the silting up of the smaller port in the town of Ostia. Portus now lies under Rome's Fiumicino airport. The island adjacent to it contains mausoleums.

Matidius Patrunius and Scribonius Amerinus are recorded as having been Roman senators in the approximate period in which this novel is set. There is no record that either of them ever met Prima.

A *Temple of Isis* has not yet been found in the section of Herculaneum that has so far been excavated, but it is probable that there was a temple which remains covered by modern houses. A painting was found by archaeologists in Herculaneum, and it depicts a Temple of Isis in the town with the head priest standing on the top step of the entry to the temple interior, looking down at the priests below. One priest performs the lighting of a ceremonial fire. Flamingos and Ibises can also be seen in the painting.

At the time of the eruption of Vesuvius, the Egyptian goddess, Isis, had become very popular with many in Rome where there were also temples dedicated to her.

Eventually, with the coming of Christianity, the figure of Isis transitioned into that of the Virgin Mary.

Excavations have revealed ownership details of some of the establishments depicted in the novel such as:

Sextus Patulchus Felix (Baker)
Aulus Fuferus (Fruit Seller)
Vennidius Ennychus Owner, the Black Saloon.

Houses/Villas in Herculaneum which also feature include:

Piso Villa dei Papyri
The House of the Beautiful Courtyard
The House of the Stags
The House of the Mosaic Atrium

Military Guard Barracks
Rome

It has been known for some time that there was a military barracks located adjacent to Rome's city wall. Recently, archaeologists found another, underneath the path of a planned new modern subway station. It is thought to have been the house of a commanding officer with accommodation attached for praetorian guards. Mosaics and other finds indicate that it was a building of considerable quality. Its occupation is thought to have been at or probably just after the date of the time of Titus.

It is possible that there are more of these barracks yet to be found by excavators.

Egypt

Following the death of Cleopatra, Egypt came under Roman rule. She had been of Greek descent, not Egyptian, but the two cultures had already become successfully meshed.

It is interesting today to study remaining examples of statues from that time which combine both Egyptian and Roman characteristics, so it appears that the culture at the time similarly accepted Roman influences.

The Roman Prefect of Egypt during the period of this novel is recorded as being Prefect Cassianus Priscus. His daughter, Vita, in this novel is a fictitious character as are the secret agents under his command.

REFERENCE MATERIAL

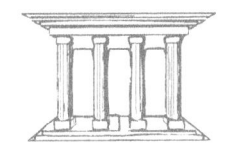

Deiss, Joseph. J. *Herculaneum: Italy's Buried Treasure,* Harper & Row, New York, Updated Edition, *1985.*
Wallace-Hadrill, Andrew. *Herculaneum: Past & Future,* Frances Lincoln Ltd., London, 2011.

GLOSSARY

Albergo	Hotel
Amphora	A vessel made of pottery
Atrium	Main reception room of a house
Award of Valour	Roman award for military bravery
Basilica	A large public building
Campania	A country region south of Rome
Cardo	A north-south street
Centurion	An officer in the Roman army
Curia	Senate House
Decumanus	A main street
Dominus	Master
Domina	Lady/Mistress

Gladius	Sword used by Roman soldiers
Palaestra	Large sports area
Plautus	Roman playwright
Portico	A porch
Saloon	Reception room
Salve	Hello or goodbye
Samian ware	Quality Roman pottery tableware
Subura	A poor area of ancient Rome
Thermopolium	Street food shop
Toga	Roman long, formal male attire
Tribune	High ranking Roman military officer
Wings	Part of a theatre backstage
Venus	Goddess of Love